MW00767840

FOOLS IN NEW ENGLAND

An Alec Black & Marie Quilby Mystery

By
Angelo A. Fazio

Bookman LLC
Publishing & Marketing

Providing Quality, Professional Author Services

www.bookmanmarketing.com

ISBN: 1-59453-272-9

"Who" was behind Richard's death?
"What" was the cause for Alec's pursuit?
"Where" was Marie when Alec needed her most?
"When" did Alec decide it was time?
"Why" was Rita shot and Marie concerned?

Marie managed to keep her wits about herself and the situation. Who knew Marie's ignited fury was capable of neutralizing the most knowledgeable experts in the field? Her abilities were what many would consider a deadly force.

How was Alec to know how far Lieutenant Bill Rockwell would go, especially after Captain Sybinski, of the seventh police precinct, reprimanded his authority?

"What the hell were you thinking, Sargent Fuz?" Bill said, as he stood behind his desk reaching for his black coffee, smoking from the steam. "This is out of your league, Fuz. Do I make myself clear?"

"Crystal clear," Sargent Fuz, of the second shift, responded.

Alec Black knew exactly where he was going and knew his life was in danger. But he's been there before and knew the consequences. "I knew I'd stumble across the truth," Alec thought, as he figured out Professor Johnson's position at the State college.

"Why that Sumbitch," Mr. B grunted, knowing quite well he was on the right track. Alec Black, better known as "Mr. B", had no client this time. Was Alec compelled to pursue what he thought was evidence, or was it his cowboy boots, he was more concerned about?

My thanks go to my beautiful wife Gerrie for her
support.
My daughter Lori who edited my novel and also my
dear friend Pat who inspired me to write.

A quote from, Gee,
I wonder who?
"A friendship is often more important than a passionate
romance"
Watch for Angelo Fazio's next novel
"Ruthless New England"
In a book store near you

My Brother Joe, a well known international musician and lyric writer has not only helped sponsor, "Fools In New England" but also wrote a special song entitled "My Marie". For details on "My Marie" and many other well known hits from Fazio Farm Record studio, simply write Joe Fazio at: faziofarmrecords@aol.com.

Chapter I

The month of November was extremely crisp and cold. It was colder than as far back as the winter of 1968, the year we had the NorEaster. It was a terrible and shocking storm that crippled and paralyzed major cities from the tip of Maine, to the Southern coast of Rhode Island.

Yet, here I was pumping fuel into my brand-new Ford V-10 pickup, at the local gas station.

As I stood motionless, pumping fuel, I felt the clear crisp air with each breath I took. It hurt down deep inside my chest. The wind surged around my fingers and turned them white. But, of course, squeezing the handle of the gas nozzle didn't help. It was so cold that it felt as if I was holding an icicle. When I left the house, I thought I was wearing adequate clothing for New England weather. Boy, was I wrong! Man, it was brutally cold for what I was wearing, too damn cold.

As the fueling of my furious V-10 gas guzzler came to a stop, I observed something very peculiar. After I placed the nozzle back into the pump-housing I noticed that my right hand, the hand which had held the nozzle, obviously had melted something red. As I looked down at the pavement, I had discovered that whatever the red liquid was, it had now dripped onto my right Alligator cowboy boot. "Sumbitch," I muttered, somewhat irritated. Not thinking, I reached for my sale receipt, from the little window next to the credit card slot. It was then, and only then, that I realized that the red liquid may not be from me, or from the ketchup of my french fries I had just devoured. I thought, "Could this be blood? Human blood? Maybe it may have something to do with foul play?" Others would dismiss this as something trivial. However, as a detective, I became very suspicious. That's how my apprehensive mind works.

My name is Alec, Alec Black. Better know as "Alec" or "Mr. B" outside the office. I collected my receipt, now riddled with redness, placed it on the napkin, which I used for my fries and drove off. I drove off for about fifty yards and decided to turn back to the fueling station. I needed to know what was on my hand and boot.

As I walked into the little gas station convenience variety store, the floors were wet and dirty. They were soiled with oil and grit, from consumers going in and out. It was the typical traffic one sees in New England during the late fall and winter months. To my left, there were two young boys, around thirteen or fourteen years of age. They were dressed in jeans, sneakers, and long sleeve plaid shirts. They were not at all dressed for the temperatures outside. They stood there glancing at "adult" magazines, giggling, like they were getting away with something. I wondering to myself, "Why aren't they in school?" To my right, there were several rows of shelves, and at the rear of the store was a blond person's head. From a distance, it appeared as though a head was resting on top of the shelf, but of course I knew the individual was standing behind it. The individual was obviously viewing rows of frozen foods in refrigerators, deciding what to purchase.

I continued towards the counter using caution, because of the slippery wet floors. When I reached the counter, a scuzzy, non-shaven guy, with holey sneakers, sweatpants, sweatshirt, and about sixty pounds over weight, said, "EXCUSE ME! I WAS HERE BEFORE YOU!"

"Yes, yes you were" I replied, and used my favorite clause, "No problem." I could see why he took a while getting to the counter. He was nearly out of breath. I smiled and gestured with my slightly sticky red right hand, and said, "After you."

When the scuzzy man's sale activity was complete, I approached the attendant. After reading the name on his shirt, I showed him my I.D., stated my name and asked, "Who was the last person on fueling pump number seven, Bob?"

Bob, the attendant said, "What do I look like, a know it all?"

I replied, "No, you look like an intelligent, responsible, fuel station attendant, that could use another employee to help out stocking the shelves, while you tend to customers at the register." With that statement, Bob smiled and was a little more willing to answer the question.

As we conversed about why I needed to know, he became interested himself, then opened the register drawer, looking to find if there were any paper bills or change covered with blood. To his surprise, he found a ten dollar bill with a smidgen of redness. I then commenced to give him another ten for that one, when he said, "Information like this should be worth, let's see, twenty bucks, don't you think?" I stated my favorite phrase again, "No problem" and gave him the twenty requested. I then turned and walked towards the door. As I continued walking, I noticed his reflection on the store window. He had a huge smile on his face as he placed the twenty dollar bill into the drawer, then removed ten dollars, from the register drawer into his pocket.

"Ten bucks, for a possible lead on a homicide; any day in my book!" I muttered. How could he be so fooled, I gave him the twenty requested, and yet he had to replace the ten I took, back into the drawer. Where do they find employees today?

Chapter II

Our successful Private Detective Agency, has been located at the corner of Hawaii Boulevard and Lanai Lane for the last twenty-two years, with no plans in moving. Marie Quilby is my partner. She's one of the best investigators any detective could have as an associate. Marie always arrived at the office three minutes before nine every morning. She is very punctual like that.

When Marie was seven years old, her parents were both killed in a train accident while visiting her grandparents during Oktoberfest, in Germany. Marie somehow miraculously survived and underwent an extremely emotional period of grief. She was raised by her very proper English grandmother and her exceptionally tough German grandfather. Her grandfather was also grieving his daughter's and Son-in-Law's death. The combination of genes and circumstances of her parent's sudden death, resulted in the person Marie is today. Marie always dresses very beautifully. She's about 5'8", has light brown hair, brown eyes, very shapely, and extremely intelligent, with just a hint of a German accent, picked up from when she was a child. I've known Marie for many years, even before we started our detective agency together. She's had my attention since High School. Why I never got involved with Marie, is totally beyond me. She really is everything any man would ever want and need, perhaps too much for some.

Sure we go out for dinner and socialize. Marie's single, and smart, smart enough not to get hitched. Of course, I've always admired Marie, who wouldn't? I know she respects me, just as I respect her. That, I think, has been the key to our successfully Private Investigation business.

Today was Tuesday and it was her turn to bring the coffee, breakfast croissants, and the morning newspaper. As I walked into the office, she stared directly into my eyes and said, "Good Morning, Alec." I returned the greeting, "Good morning, Marie."

As we sipped coffee, and ate our croissants in complete silence, the only thing you'd hear was the turning of pages from the morning paper. The office was usually silent, not only because we'd be reading and digesting information, but also digesting our favorite morning treats. It was twenty-two years of harmony, and we liked it.

Shortly after, we would finish reading the paper, usually around 9:30, we'd discuss the current events and also our clients. However, when Marie finished and set the paper down this morning, she asked, "Where were you last night? I waited thirty minutes at 'Peters Pub', had my usual Samuel Adams, and you never showed. It's not like you at all Alec. What's up? Would you like to talk about it?"

"Yeah, Marie, I do," I replied.

We were able to speak with one another, without holding back anything, even things down to the smallest detail. "I was hoping to find something in this morning's paper, something having to do with a slaying. But maybe there's nothing to what happened last night. Nothing after all."

"What do you mean?" Marie replied, in her sexy German accent.

I explained the whole episode and how it involved me, my cowboy boot, the ten dollar bill, and the receipt from fueling. Each with a sample of blood suspected drops on them.

"Marie, am I being silly, or does this look suspicious? It may not even be blood at all. Should I continue to pursue what I feel may be evidence or shall I just drop the whole thing?"

Her response was as I expected. "If there's anything shady about what's before us, Alec, we'll get to the bottom of it. That's what's we do. That's why we're Private Investigators," Marie said.

Usually we get paid three hundred dollars per day, plus expenses by clients to investigate. However, I had no client and since it was my hand that melted the bloody ice from the fuel pump handle, I felt compelled to pursue. "Who's blood could it be? Was there foul play? What fool or 'Fools in New England' would leave incriminating evidence on a gas pump nozzle?" That's my case and it's been bugging me for the last seventeen hours. Marie and I conversed the subject quite a while, when she suggested bringing it to the attention of Lieutenant William Rockwell, at the 7th precinct.

We finished our conversation and went downstairs into the foyer, got bundled up and prepared ourselves for the blast of arctic cold air as we opened the front door.

Chapter III

Marie's wheels for transportation, are really cool. She shows real class. Just three months ago, I was asked to help select the interior for a new Dodge Viper she was purchasing. I suggested the works- black leather seats, with every possible option available, including dual exhaust. After all, you didn't want to skimp with the extras, when it came to sitting in an $80,000 destiny super sports car. And believe me, today, when she sat behind the wheel, you knew she was destined to own one. She looked absolutely drop dead gorgeous sitting there. Beneath her black faux fur over coat, was a striking gray two piece outfit. Her skirt revealed her long beautiful legs and nude color nylons. "God, she looked beautiful," I thought to myself, as I admired her while sitting beside her on the passenger side.

Marie down shifted as we approached the end of Hawaii Boulevard to turn right onto the opposite end of Lanai Lane. You could tell she was very capable of harnessing whatever gusto, the candy apple red Viper had to offer. We could have used a machine such as this three years ago during a car chase which ended with a roll over. But that's another story.

When we arrived at the police station, I went around to open the driver's door. I guess I came from the old school, I really don't see too much of that polite stuff anymore. However for me, it was common place. I felt it showed manners, elegance, style and appreciation.

9

As Marie got out of the sports car, I extended my hand. Marie didn't by any means, need any man's hand, but as I said, she has class, and reached out. I shut the door and we went into the police station.

An unfamiliar Sargent was behind the caged counter. His name plate said Sgt. Steven Brand. Before looking up at us, he apparently had unfinished paper work from the previous person, who was nowhere in sight. We figured either Sargent Brand was new, or he was still thinking about the powdered donut he had just made mysteriously disappear. The powdered sugar from his donut was embarrassing. Parts of his uniform, especially the black tie was covered in white.

"May I help you?" the Sargent asked, addressing his question to Marie.

"Yes," she replied. "We'd like to speak with Lieutenant Rockwell, in the Homicide division."

"Who, may I ask, wants to see him?"

I interrupted and said, "Tell him, Alec Black and Ms. Quilby would like to see him."

Sgt. Brand continued, "Is there something I can do?"

"Yes," I said, "There is donut powder on your uniform. Your appearance is a direct reflection on Captain Sybinski and his entire 7th precinct. Clean up the mess, look sharp Sargent," I said in a pleasant tone of voice.

He informed Lieutenant Rockwell of our presence, as I apologized to Marie for interrupting. Then with my evidence, we advanced to Lieutenant Rockwell's office.

I knocked on the Lieutenant's door. "Come on in Captain Black, the door is open."

Lieutenant Bill Rockwell and I go way back, back to when we both served in the military together. "I see you brought the lovely Ms. Quilby, it's always a pleasure. Please sit down. What can I do for you, Captain Black and Marie?" Bill asked.

I proceeded to explain to Bill, what I considered to be evidence and my assumption that a possible homicide may have taken place. At first Bill thought it was "Hog wash," but as we went on conversing, his attitude began to change.

There was one sentence, which Marie added, as we were concluding our visit. She said, "Lieutenant Rockwell, what if Mister B, does have evidence towards a true Homicide, and what if your precinct doesn't address the issue at hand? This fool would actually be mocking you thinking he got away with murder."

With her statement, I also added, "At least check out the DNA (Deoxyribonucleic Acid) at the lab. When Marie and I resolve the issues, the blood samples will be here in your lab and not destroyed by some kid cleaning the gas pumps, where the alleged blood was originally found."

Then Marie added, "Alec and I will publicly state how you got involved with our operation and apprehended the individual or individuals involved."

With that, the Lieutenant gave us the thumbs up and we left the office. As we walked towards the front door, I couldn't help but notice Sgt. Brand had changed his tie. "Alec," Marie said, "check that out." I grinned.

After talking in the viper for a few minutes, about our next destination, Marie started the engine, then drove off. We were on our way to the gas station where the blood first appeared. You could tell Marie enjoyed traveling in the sports car. The way she shifted, said it all. It seemed like we were gliding instead of driving down the streets.

The location of the gas station was some distance away from the precinct going around town, so I asked, "Marie, would you be interested in Peter's Pub tonight?" Marie had just finished up one of her cases she had brought to the office. We were to meet at Peter's Pub last night to celebrate the conclusion of the case, when all this came up. Hopefully she would agree to go out tonight, since we never went last night. I was looking forward to having dinner and a few drinks in special company, instead of the usual. I usually spend my evenings pretty much alone. My home is located outside city limits, in a wooded area. No one has ever stepped foot in my fairly new four car garage colonial home. Once, two years ago, I invited Marie, however she had a prior engagement. Usually, I wander the house sipping wine or beer and eating TV dinners, while watching television. Going out with Marie would have certainly been a welcomed change.

Her response about Peter's Pub was "no". She told me that she had plans already.

As she was working on the last case, she had bumped into an old dear friend, Jimmy Johnson.

Jimmy was definitely top notch. His family came from old money. No matter where Jimmy went, people showed admiration towards him and his inheritance. He lost both parents also, in a plane crash ten years ago, on their way to England.

Jimmy, their only son, inherited their Morgan horse farm and the entire estate. His education in management and finances, have continued to keep the late Johnson's estate in great standings through out sixty percent of the horse racing arenas. If Marie wound up hitching with Jimmy, it would be no surprise.

Since they had made arrangements to go out tonight, I figured, I'd watch "Mysterious Ways" on the tube at 9:00. I look forward to watching certain programs every week and "Mysterious Ways" is one of them.

Angelo A. Fazio

Chapter IV

We finally reached the gas station parking lot, where I first acquired the blood stains. There were two police cruisers and one crime van upon the scene, gathering evidence. Apparently, Lieutenant Bill Rockwell had dispersed the homicide unit to search the alleged crime scene. This also meant Marie and I couldn't cross the yellow enclosed perimeter, in fear of contaminating a crime scene. So, we decided to walk the outside of the yellow plastic taped line, instead.

From a distance, you could see Bob, the attendant of the little variety store, becoming very upset. His quota for recommended fuel sales had dropped considerably since the police got involved.

I pointed out to Marie where pump number seven was, and both Marie and I started our investigation. Marie started looking for security surveillance cameras in the adjacent parking lots. Security cameras have a very good depth and width perception. Her goal was to find cameras outside of the yellow taped crime line, which the homicide unit put up, and locate cameras aimed in the general direction of pump number seven. If she got lucky finding one, she'd have to ask the abutting business' permission to borrow the video cameras to obtain evidence.

"Who knows? We may find important film footage, perhaps something out of the ordinary, and in this case, I hoped we would," I thought. I started combing the area for spectators, curious people who may have seen something unusual, or something out of place. Working the public for any possible clues was my skill. I was looking for a vehicle or person with disturbing blood stains. Perhaps someone had seen such a person?

After mingling with the public asking questions for a while, some time had passed. It was getting close to 4:00 pm and around Northern New England it becomes rather dark by 4:30 during the winter months. So, Marie and I had to wrap up our surveillance and regroup at the office on Wednesday morning at 9:00 am with my notes and Marie with her camera gear, we packed up and left the area. The Homicide unit remained with headlights, drop lights, flashlights, whatever light they had available. Once Homicide started investigating a crime scene, it was very important to have fresh evidence.

I, for one, didn't envy their occupation. I've seen shift after shift, dressed in their white one-piece jumpers, continuing to work at a crime scene for days. Can you imagine the sweat that occurs in a one-piece jumper on a real hot summer day? You gotta respect them.

Marie, dropped me off at the office, where I had left my truck, then she drove off to prepare for her date with Jimmy. Before I decided to leave for home, I went upstairs with my notes, while things were fresh in my mind and I decided to continue working, entering information acquired from the crime scene, into the computer.

It was now a little after 6:00 pm on Tuesday, and I wasn't a bit tired, and I had someone who worked the second shift at homicide, "Fuzzy". He's my oldest son, from my separated wife. Fuz got his name from me when he was in his teens. Where I had a receding hairline, he continued to have hair down to his shoulders. He liked long hair, so I started calling him Fuzzy. I think the only time he cut it was when he got involved with criminal law.

Anyway, Fuz worked the second shift and since he was my son, at times, he would try helping me on cases. I had nowhere to go and nothing to do, until 9:00 pm, when "Mysterious Ways" was on television. So, I figured I'd visit Fuz back at the crime site.

I didn't waste any time getting back to the crime scene. I had to know from Fuz, if the attendant, Bob, at the gas station, had video footage of pump number seven that the police collected from inside the store. Also, we needed to find out if it was a man or woman who entered the store to pay cash for gas.

Fuz was at the site patrolling the perimeter, as the second shift continued gathering evidence. He greeted me as I walked towards him. I explained why I was there and what I was doing. He then looked at the police log reports, accumulated during the day shift. "Yes, we have the security camera with tapes," he said. "It was one of the first things we gathered on the roster, according to this report."

"Fuz, is there any way I could take a glimpse?" I asked.

"No way, absolutely not," he replied, as he went to get the camera. Fuz then placed the whole camera on the air compressor box, just inside the yellow tape crime barrier. Then he went inside for a cup of coffee and a cupcake. I chuckled to myself when I saw him in the store through the lit interior. Him and his cupcakes, he loved cupcakes like I loved croissants. "Yeah, that's my son!" I said to myself. I put my crime gloves on and started pushing the fast forward buttons on the video camera.

Fuz was gone for about fifteen or twenty minutes, then started to return. I could see him through the store window. As he turned and walked towards the door, the video had just started to show something peculiar. I slowed the cameras down to regular play, viewing a 1988 blue vintage Ford pickup truck. I knew my Fords. I had Fords since I was 16 years old. I also knew it was hunting season and there was no reason for me to suspect anything suspicious, with a deer in the back, but too many things were very coincidental.

I wondered if Bill would pick out the deer? The individual pumping gas was so covered with blood and winter clothing, it was very difficult to make him out. I managed to recognize his hat. I nearly purchased a similar hat at the local discount store myself. The passenger appeared to be a white male with long blond hair, shoulder length. I continued the film again in fast forward. The film showed fifteen minutes between the blue pickup truck and the time that I had arrived in my truck. There was no other vehicle in between. That gave me a very good idea of how cold it was last night, and also that the blood wasn't contaminated with other DNA.

Fuz reached out his hand for the camera, just as I shut the camera off. I commended him for not showing, or telling, me anything about the case and said, "Goodnight, Fuz."

"Sure Dad," he said. "Have a good night."

I headed back to the office. I felt comfortable, now that I had something to work with. As I drove back, I kept thinking about the clothing the guy on the tape was wearing. There was something missing. There was the deer in the rear of the pickup, but no bright orange clothing, or clothing that hunters normally wear.

"Was this a missing piece of my puzzle? Yes!" I said to myself, "I got you now!"

One piece at a time. Marie and I had an excellent reputation, one that other private Investigators admired. It was our ability to solve the worst possible crimes. Under that very clause, "one piece at a time" I went back to the office and added the fresh information into the computer, before I forgot any part of it, then started on my way home.

Angelo A. Fazio

Chapter V

After drying myself off from taking a shower, I wrapped a towel around my waist and started supper. The canned tuna didn't seem to have much taste. So I added more mayonnaise, changing the flavor. "There, that'll do it," I thought. Here it was ten minutes before my Tuesday night television show "Mysterious Ways" and my tuna sandwich tasted like something a homeless person would find in a trash barrel. "I should have probably stuck with the TV dinners," I muttered. "At least I knew what to expect."

I made some popcorn in the micro, gathered a six-pack of beer and sat on my favorite $399 recliner. I had two recliners, one was for guests but, it remained empty since the day I got it. I was preparing to have a peaceful relaxing television show night when, suddenly, the phone rang. "Damn it, now what!" I considered letting the machine take it. But, like a rat in a maze addressing a bell, in scientific research, I picked up the cell phone by my chair.

"Hello?" I said Controlling my irritation, I said. "Who is it?" I heard sobbing on the opposite end of the phone.

"Who is it?" I insisted. Still no answer, just sobbing.

"If I don't hear a name within the count of three, I'm going to hang up!" I said.

Finally, I heard a very weak "Alf". The voice was female and there is only one person who calls me that.

"Marie?" I asked. "What's going on? Why are you crying?"

I have known Marie for many years and I have never heard her cry. Something must be terribly wrong for Marie to even call me at home.

Instinctively I asked, "Are you ok?" I then heard a jarring thud come over the phone line.

"Where are you Marie?" I continued to ask in desperation.

"Where are you Marie?"

"I'm okay," she said with a long and drawn out voice.

"I'm at the office. Please hurry!" Again her voice was crackling and getting weaker and quieter.

Immediately, I skyrocketed off the recliner, threw the half eaten tuna sandwich and popcorn in the trash container, slipped on a pair of jogging shoes, a bathrobe, and flew out the door. I tried desperately to keep her on the telephone as I accelerated down my long driveway. I spared no horses, reaching a speed of 140 mph, on Route 95. As I showed no mercy for the V-10 engine, I couldn't help but wonder what could possibly have happened to Marie. I continued down the road and before I knew it, I arrived at the office.

"Holy crap!!" I said aloud, as I reached the top of the office stairs. I found Marie lying in a pool of blood. She wasn't crying, she was struggling and gasping, having trouble breathing!

"Don't you dare die on me, Marie!" I shouted, as she lay before me, in and out of consciousness. All misty-eyed, I couldn't imagine my life without her.

"Marie, you'll be alright, you'll be alright," I repeated and reassured her as she continued deeper into unconsciousness.

I didn't know whether or not she had called 911. She wasn't able to answer, and I wasn't going to wait around to find out either. With a sudden escalation of adrenaline, I whisked Marie up from the floor, into my arms, and ran her out of the building. I then placed her tenderly in the front seat of my truck, and ran around to the drivers side.

When I got behind the steering wheel, I placed it in drive and pushed the accelerator to the floor then kept it there. The hospital was just two miles down the street, on the way I kept trying to speak with Marie. "You're a strong woman," I said. "Marie, you'll be okay. You'll be okay." I was sure she'd be okay, I convinced myself.

We reached the emergency section of the hospital's parking lot within a couple minutes. Leaving the truck running, I ran around to the passenger side and vigorously carried Marie out of the truck, clutched her tightly as I ran towards the big glass entrance doors, shouting for help along the way. Four nurses came out to help. We placed Marie on the gurname and I continued holding her hand as she was scooted directly into Emergency Room.

The only thing I knew for sure was that Marie had been shot. She had been shot somewhere in the upper left chest. "Who? Who the hell would want to shoot Marie?" I wondered. A primitive surge of anger emerged with a smug expression on my face, causing me to get red and it clouded my thinking. "Was it Jimmy? No, no," I said to myself. "Calm down. When Marie comes out of it, I'll have all the answers." But I just couldn't help thinking, "If that sorry sumbitch had anything to do with this, I'd hurt Jimmy bad, really bad!"

I asked the nurses if I may have a coffee from their coffee maker, seeing I left everything at home, including my wallet and cash.

"Sure!" Nurses Lori and Katie said, almost simultaneously and they then continued on with their hospital work.

I sat in the waiting room anxiously sipping coffee waiting for news of Marie's progress. Four hours had slipped by. It was now 1:00 am. Worriedly, the doctor came out. He had that look that doctors have as he approached. I asked, "How is she doing doctor?"

He gave me the same bull crap story, I see on television. He looked straight into my eyes and said, "We're doing the best we can."

After hearing that, I lost my composure. I got in his face and went nose to nose, eyeball to eyeball, and said, "If anything happens to Marie, I am holding you directly responsible! Now go back into that emergency room, where you call yourselves gods in, and don't come out until you have something positive to tell me. I will be waiting right here! Am I making myself clear, Doctor?!"

The frightened doctor didn't say a word. He turned and re-entered the emergency room, and shut the door behind him. I then sat back down on the soft chair and waited. A few minutes had past when I noticed the nurses looking at me, giggling as there eyes focused on me.

"What, what is it?" I asked. I then realized that I was still wearing my bathrobe. It had apparently come undone and that I forgot that I had put nothing on underneath. "No wonder the doctor didn't say a word and just walked away." I thought back and I remembered that I got out of the shower then I got so involved with my TV show. When I got the phone call from Marie, I totally lost all reasoning.

I turned opposite the nurses, closed my robe and I apologized for my appearance. "How could I have left the house like this?" I thought. "Imagine, I howled at Sargent Brand because he had a little donut powder on his tie, and here I was, with my little pa`dingle exposed! What a night!" I thought, as I lowered and shook my head.

It was quarter to 3:00am and the Doctor came out again with the same look. Softly I mumbled, "Oh, no." It was the same look he gave me earlier. He walked closer, and he motioned to me with his hands, like a police officer slowing vehicles down from speeding. He came closer then closer and said, "She's pulling through." I sighed relief. "But," he said aggressively "she's not to be disturbed, under any circumstances! Am I making, myself, clear?!"

I thanked him politely. The doctor then said, "Did I have any other choice? The look you gave me was as if she didn't pull through, you'd kill me." I apologized to the Doctor again. But, I think he may have been right. I may have!

Since I couldn't do anything there at the hospital anyway, I told the nurses I'd be at home. I gave them my home phone number, in the event there were any changes in Marie's health, and then left.

The following morning I slept until 9:00am. I called the nurse's station and they told me Marie was awake and they said, if I wanted to see her, to come right on in. I thanked them and hung-up the phone.

I got cleaned up then dressed and managed to make it to Mike's Diner for breakfast. Once I have my breakfast, I usually feel really great. I paid the waitress and left to see Ms. Quilby.

Even in a hospital bed, Marie looked pretty hot. I smiled and said "Good morning." She replied, "Good morning, Mister B. What's this I hear? You gave the nurses your home phone number? What do you need a date or something?" She chuckled with an expression of pain on her face.

"Shall we conduct an office meeting here in bed?" I asked jokingly.

"We shouldn't mix business with pleasure," she replied. Then we hugged.

"Glad you made it, Marie. The office would never have been the same without you. Do you feel up to filling me in on what happened? Or is it too soon? I don't want you getting upset so soon after this terrible experience."

That's when Marie started, "Wait till I get out of here and back on my feet! That sorry bastard!! He's going to get his!"

"Who?" I impatiently asked. "Jimmy? That sorry Sumbitch!"

"No, No, No, you dummy," Marie said. "Jimmy canceled out last night. He said something came up. So, I decided to start my research with the surveillance cameras that I had managed to collect. You know, the cameras from both sides of the adjacent parking lots? Well, I decided to go back to our office. I needed to enhance the video with our equipment in the back room. I just got into the office foyer, when suddenly, as I was shutting the front door, this guy in a truck, comes out from nowhere and plugs me in the chest. I barely managed to get upstairs to reach the phone by the office door because my cell phone was still in the Viper. I wasn't sure if the shooter would still be there outside to shoot me again, so I decided not to go for the phone in the car."

"By any chance Marie, was the truck blue?" I asked.

"Yes," she said surprisingly, "how did you know?"

I then brought Marie up to date on what information I had gathered from going back to the fueling station.

"Listen, Marie," I said, "they tell me you'll be able to leave tomorrow. I realize that you'll probably want to get right back to work, but I want to see you take it easy for the next couple of days, at least. Tomorrow I'll be in the office, and I can try piecing together as much of the puzzle as possible and gather as many details as I can." Marie smiled and lit up the room. I held and kissed her hand for a couple seconds, then headed towards the door.

The elevator ride down from Marie's room was very quick. The lack of sleep, combined with my age, made me feel a little dizzy as I stepped off.

"Heck," I thought to myself, "when I was younger, nothing bothered me. The heavy assault of gunfire upon the helicopter, interrupted my entire life and style of living. It wasn't till I had several lead holes, plugged into my stomach, by way of a machine gun, during the latter part of my enlistment duty in Vietnam, that caused my whole life to take a wicked dip and turn."

I continued towards the street through the huge glass revolving doors. This was a very nice Hospital. The lobby looked more like a hotel. At times, I've even had lunch in the cafeteria. I knew for sure, they make a better tuna sandwich than I do.

I continued to the Police station, prior to going to the video technician analysis department, which was located just behind the police building. I was interested in knowing whether any prints, other than my own, showed up at the crime scene.

According to Lieutenant Rockwell, there were hundreds and hundreds of overlapping prints, on the gas handle which made it difficult to decipher and to single out just one individual set of prints, prints were almost impossible. I really wasn't anticipating any one singled out prints, anyway. But, I had to ask.

As I thought back to Tuesday night, when I viewed the video from Fuzzy's shift, at the gas station, I remembered that the guy that I saw in the video was wearing gloves, while pumping gas. I decided not to mention anything to Bill that I had already watched the film, I did not want to get my son in trouble. I then said, "Are you going to view the video tapes with me?"

He replied "Yeah, in the screening room. I'm going over there now. Want to come along?"

"Sure," I said.

Bill always appeared agreeable. I've really never had any problems with him or any other cops. We always seem to have gotten along. Unlike what they lead you to believe on television, or even in some books people read, the Police really are there for you.

Heck, in the past, Bill and I even discussed possible scenarios "for crying out loud" (an old saying I've heard somewhere in my past).

Everything we viewed, other than what I saw with the blue truck, was unimportant. However, I was kind of surprised when Bill didn't halt the film on the blue truck with the dead deer. He usually picks up on everything. He didn't see it, so I didn't mention it.

The next stop was the DNA department. I asked the Lieutenant if he was going with me, and he said, "Go on ahead, Alec, I'll check it out after this meeting with Captain Sybinski. The captain wants to know why I dispatched the homicide division over to the gas station Tuesday night."

"Really?" I said. "Tell the captain to 'go suck an egg'! Soon he'll have egg white all over himself! I swear at times Bill, I don't understand why the captain fights and questions your every move. I don't know if

Marie getting shot last night, and if the bloody gas station pump nozzle are even linked together. But I tell you Bill, if the captain drops the ball, he'll hear it from me for letting this Sumbitch go! Anyway, see you later, Bill. Oh, and by the way, do ya wanna tip a couple tonight, at Pete's Pub?" I asked.

"Alec, I'll have to get back to you on that. The kids have been acting up and my wife wants me to nip it in the bud. You know, what I mean, 'wait till your father comes home, your father will straighten you out'. You know, that sort of thing," Bill said.

"Actually Bill," I said, "I know exactly what you mean. If you need to get away for a break, just leave a message on my answering machine." Bill thanked me.

I proceeded to go to the DNA lab, in the south wing of the police station. I then stepped outside onto the crosswalk bridge, in order to get to the next building. Suddenly, a gust of freezing cold, raw wind reared its ugly head.

In New England, once the cold season starts, it's sort of like a yo-yo. If you wait a few minutes, the weather will change in any direction. From cold to colder, or from cold to windy and colder, or from cold to windy, cloudy and colder, or from cold to unbearable! At times I ask myself, "What am I doing here in New England? I should be down South doing the same type of work, but not freezing my snapper off." But, what can I do? It's been almost a decade since my wife and I have separated, and now we're getting a divorce. She wants everything, even the very air I breathe.

Trevor and two other technicians ran the entire DNA lab area. Trevor is the guy I wanted to see. Fuz introduced me to him, in years past, so as always, I went directly to see him. I walked uninterruptedly, down the corridor. I saw my gas receipt, the ten dollar bill, and my right cowboy boot, enclosed in a temperature control environment, wrapped in a special see through bag. It's today's modern technology, but I call it 'Mo-tech'.

"Good afternoon, Trevor," I said. "Whazzup, with my boot and my receipt? Anything promising?"

"Hey, Mister B, whazzup?" he responded. I asked Trevor, if my 'boot was made for walking' yet?

"No, not yet, but give me 'til morrow. There's much more here than you think, bro."

"Surprise me, Trevor," I said. "Take your time."

"These little dabs are telling us an unusual story," Trevor added.

Trevor graduated at the top of his class. There were diplomas hanging all over his Lab. I'd be proud too if it were me. He came from Jamaica, received citizenship and worked his way up through college.

"Can you give me a hint?" I asked.

"Can no do that, bro," he said.

"Ok, Trevor, my man," I said. "No pressure from Mister B."

Naturally, I started hypothesizing Trevor's discoveries. "What did he find?" I wondered, as we talked and talked about the samples of blood. It was almost time to call it quits for the day. Needless to say,

I was disappointed. Almost 42 hours had passed and still no major evidence.

I went up to see Marie again to say hi, knowing that she was probably going stir crazy. She was a very active and a very determined woman. I figured I'd give her something to contemplate about while she was confined to her room at the hospital. Sure enough, when I arrived to her room, she wanted me to take her home. I said, I couldn't do that, but I'd meet her half way. "Marie," I said, "I'll take you out to dinner down stairs in the Cafeteria, okay?"

"Okay," she said, "Anything! Just get me out of here!"

I helped her out of the bed, stood her up, and tied the back of her little open Johnny. However, before helping put the bottoms on, I said, "My, my, Marie." And I told Marie how really cute her little butt was. I then helped set her into the wheel chair. We wheeled off for dinner, at the exquisite cafeteria to dine.

Marie has always had such a positive outlook on life. Her outlook is always cheerful and happy, no matter what the circumstances are.

I left Marie at the table, while I went to the cafeteria rail, getting her what she yearned: meatloaf, mashed potatoes, and a nice green salad, with just a touch of Italian dressing. Once Marie sets her mind on something, she usually never vacillated. She was a very focused woman. I thought, "Soon she'd be back in the office, and things would be back to normal."

During dinner, I asked if she wanted me to pick up the Viper, and leave it in the parking lot for when she comes out of the hospital. Or, if she would rather have me pick her up with it. Marie chose me picking her up. But, come to find out, they don't let you leave the hospital, unless you have a driver anyway. I also mentioned to her that it was her turn to pick up the croissants, coffee, and newspaper, when she came back to the office. But, of course I was just kidding, I'd rather get the treats because of her temporary disabled condition.

She laughed and laughed when I said disabled condition. Then suddenly, she reached over the side of the table, grasped the collar of my shirt, and gave me a great big tug leaning my face next to hers, and she gave me a fantastic kiss on the lips.

Oooooo man! I loved it. I guess I looked pretty flushed and stunned, because the Chinese couple that was sitting next to our table were smiling and nodding, as to say they approved of that behavior.

"Marie," I asked, "is there anything else you'd like at the cafe? I, ah, gotta get some, ah, water. Water, that's it, yeah some water." Marie obviously had a way of exciting me. My animalistic instincts were becoming quite visible, as I kissed her back.

After our delightful dinner, I brought her back upstairs, into her room. I tucked her in bed, and made jokes, laughing about some insignificant topic. She needed rest, I could see. I waited until she fell asleep, then shortly after, I kissed her gently, squeezed her hand, and said goodnight. I left the hospital finally feeling up about her condition.

When I arrived at the office, back from the hospital, I just decided to stay and sleep there for the night. Marie's Viper was still outside the office, where she had left it the night she was shot. It was late, and I was extremely tired from all the day's activities. I was, as they say, 'too pooped' to even drive home. Within just a few minutes, I was 'out like a light'.

Chapter VI

I woke well rested, despite sleeping on the couch. I stretched and looked with hazed eyes into Marie's section of the office. I was totally shocked to see her side of the office in complete shambles. Suddenly, I realized that we had a visitor some time during last evening. Was I so tired that I didn't notice her office when I entered last night? I don't think so. Which only led to one other conclusion, and I don't want to go there.

I went through my triple SSS's (s—, shower, and shave) I was ready to pick up Marie with her Viper. Along the way, I picked up the usual treats.

As I approached the curb by the front entrance of the hospital, Nurse Lori had Marie in a wheelchair and was pushing her out through the hospital door. You could sense things at times, just by looking, especially when you've known a person for a long time, like I knew Marie. I could tell something was bothering Marie. When she gets in that mood, watch out because she's like a walking artillery unit ready to explode.

Marie got up from the wheelchair and walked directly towards the car, as though nothing had ever happened.

Jokingly, I said, "So Marie, how was your hotel stay?" As I shut her door and walked around to the drivers side. When I entered and sat behind the steering wheel, ready to start the engine, she turned expressionless, looking coldly into my eyes as she's done many times before. She then said, "Can you imagine Alec, Jimmy didn't even send me flowers. What an inconsiderate person."

I was about to rescue, coming to Jimmy's defense. When Marie said, "Shut up, don't say a word Alec, just drive." I had planned on bringing her home to rest, but she insisted on going to the office for a day of work, and not another word was spoken during the two mile trip to the office.

After horizontally parking the Viper in front, by the office curb, I mentioned the intruder and the condition of her side of the office. I didn't want her to be astonished by the appearance, as she entered the door.

"Alec?" Marie asked, "What's going on? What's happening? Why would anyone, in this enormous mystifying planet, be interested in our little insignificant, microscopic portion of earth?"

I had no immediate answers as to why the intruder chose our agency, so I tried to change the subject and made a silly remark, "After our croissants, Marie."

She looked around the room, trying to figure what may have been the reason as to why someone would ransack just her section and not mine. At this time, several minutes after we entered, I had my own theory, but I thought I'd be quiet and listen to her professional guesstimate. I was totally surprised when she came up with one scenario I didn't even think of.

"Marie," I said, "please, after the croissants."

Ten silent minutes had elapsed, when I felt we were back as a team again. We didn't bother straightening the office, we figured we'd do it later.

No matter how I insisted, "Relax, stay at home, read a book, take a nap." Marie was just the opposite, she was just as stern, wanting to come along investigating. "You couldn't ask for a better partner. She was tough and yet a great lady," I thought.

I drove, as we went to see Trevor, at the DNA lab. During the ride to the police station, she called Bill on the cell phone and mentioned the office break in. Bill asked, "Should my group conduct a dusting?" She responded, "No, whoever it was, I'm sure the person was wearing gloves, so, don't bother."

She notified Bill of where we were going, in the event he wanted to join us, giving him ample time to meet us there. Then terminated the connection, placing the cell phone back in her purse.

We entered the building and approached Trevor by the lab door.

"Trevor, my man," I said, as we went through the special hand shake thing, that juveniles established when greeting one another.

"What do you have for us?" I asked, as he smiled at Marie and gave her the once over, wanna do it look.

"You got some weird DNA my man," Trevor said, just as Lieutenant Bill Rockwell entered the door.

"Trevor," Bill said, "cut the jive crap, and talk like those diplomas say you do." Trevor abruptly clammed right up. Briefly.

Marie and I looked at each other in complete dismay. All these years we thought Trevor had speech impediments and couldn't speak proper English, because of some lockjaw challenges. Marie and I weren't going to let this go by, now that we knew, we smiled at each other. I planned on playing with his head every chance I got in the future. I knew Marie would do the same.

"So what do you have, Trevor?" Bill asked.

"Since I, myself, questioned the first results, Lieutenant, I performed another analysis working most the night," Trevor responded meekly, as looking for some sort of compensation. "However lieutenant, the results remained the same. I've confirmed three types of DNA. Two patterns from blood, one animal, one human. And the third was from saliva."

"Huh," I mumbled.

Then Bill asked, "What animal blood?"

"What animal blood?" Trevor said, "That's for you to find out. I haven't a clue, yet."

Since Bill missed what we saw, together, in the video room with the tapes from the fuel station, the deer in the truck, I knew what animal. "However, the human blood was something that was throwing a monkey wrench into the investigation," I thought.

Bill squinted his eyes, as to say, what the hell are you talking about. I still kept my theories under wraps. After all, it was pure speculation at this time.

Marie asked about the alleged crime scene. "Lieutenant, was there anything at the crime scene at all?"

"Yes, there was," Bill answered, "a footprint of blood under the ice. You couldn't tell there was any blood, until the boys put the special fluorescent lights on the pavement. We took the blood evidence here. Trevor said he'd have those tests done tomorrow."

Marie said aloud, "Perhaps we may have a match with today's testing with tomorrow."

"I hope so," I said, "but it's worthless without a suspect's sample of DNA."

My patience was wearing thin, "Seventy-two hours have gone by, and we didn't have a body, or a name, or anything which even suggested we had a crime. Other than Marie getting shot." With that, Marie nudged me with an elbow. "Bill, I must go," Marie said.

"I'm getting extremely tired. Could you please excuse us?"

"Sure," Bill said.

"Alec, can you take me home?" Marie asked.

"Of course, Marie, no problem," I said. "I'm sorry, I've forgot your condition and should have been more compassionate and realized earlier."

"Go, Alec, take Marie home," Bill said.

Lieutenant Rockwell remained at the lab as we departed. Marie mentioned, in the vehicle, why she had nudged me. She had remembered why she had gone to the office just before being shot. She had two videos from the parking lots, abutting the gas station. Which, in my opinion, was the reason for the intrusion at the office.

Instead of going home, I briskly drove the Viper back to Hawaii and Lanai Lane, where the office is located. We went upstairs to search for the video recorders she had so-called "borrowed".

We conversed as we searched and searched, and came to the same conclusion. The videos certainly must have had some incriminating evidence. Both cameras were missing. Perhaps there was clear evidence on film of the perpetrator. For the perpetrator to jeopardize being seen or caught, in our office, was definitely a huge risk, especially if I was sleeping on the couch. (Oops, I said I wasn't going there.)

Marie and I searched and straightened out her office area, at the same time, only to find absolutely nothing. We looked everywhere and still came up with no cameras. Again, we were at a dead end.

It was after six o'clock now and we were about ready to leave, when I asked Marie, "What happened to Jimmy, Tuesday night?"

She replied, "It's a long story and when I'm ready, I'll let you know."

As she entered her car, determined to drive home, I asked if she wanted me to escort her home. "Marie" I said "First of all, someone wants you dead. And number two Marie you're still recovering."

She replied, "Don't worry, Alf! You know, that I know how to take care of myself."

"Yes, I certainly do Marie," I responded. I got in my truck and we waved goodbye and left for home.

Chapter VII

Thursday was definitely a terrible night for TV viewing. Yet, it was a great night for going out and "doing the town". Despite my harsh and tough looking appearance, I really never had any problems getting a date when there was a need for romance. What I'd do is just go to the local "Wildfire Dance Club", in the next city, have a few drinks, share a few laughs, and get involved with a woman who shared a common interest. Naturally, I wouldn't go to bed with just anyone, but at times I almost have.

Sex really didn't play a very big part in most of my life, and dating interrupted my lifestyle. Dating meant commitment, and as a Private Investigator, I felt it wasn't fair to a relationship. Then of course there was the endless hours of working as well.

My brain always focused on challenges. However, tonight it was focused on romance. I went through my triple SSS's then got groomed, smooth, spooned, and was finally ready. I was ready to take my pride and joy out from the fourth car garage stall. It was my very nasty bucket of metal. The machine that challenged my intelligence, the machine that helped me through the grieving years of separating with my wife, Ms. Olga Carbuncle, her maiden name.

The hot rod took almost seven years to build, starting from the frame up. My son, Fuz, always hung around, helping to build it. Which, if anything ever happened to me, he'd inherit.

As the humming electric garage door opened, I turned the key, starting the fuel injected V-12. This was no ordinary classic Lincoln Continental engine. No, not by a long shot.

The engine had all the high performance, up-to-date technology, along with my cruel and savage ratio gearing, and combining engine and transmission, they certainly tortured the rear axles.

Slowly, I backed out, careful not to scratch the two thousand dollar cherry blossom red laquer finish paint job. Once outside the garage, I pushed the button, shutting the overhead garage door and rumbled loudly away to the "Wildfire".

At the Wildfire, the parking lot overflowed into the vacant grocery store parking area next door. I didn't like leaving my classic custom coupe far from the front door entrance. So, as always, when I entered the club, I'd slip Francis, one of the gigantic bouncers, a twenty dollar bill.

Francis McSheehy, was a good natured and kind hearted guy, even as a kid growing up. His parents always instilled politeness and courtesy. How he became a harsh bouncer at the Wildfire, was still a mystery to those who really knew him.

I couldn't help but notice something as I drove closer towards the front of the parking lot. There before me was a truck, similar to the one I saw on the video that Fuz had allowed me to view. I stopped near the truck and got out.

"Holy crap!" I muttered. The bed was covered with frozen blood.

I walked back to my wheels, opened the small glove box, removed my shoulder harness and my 38 caliber revolver and placed it around my shoulders. I then opened my trunk and removed a pair of my crime scene gloves, which I always carry, no matter where I go. With my pocket knife, I scraped several sections of frozen blood into an evidence bag. I then took the registration number down and returned to the car. "Was the individual that foolish?" I wondered.

I proceeded into the club, and I slipped Francis the twenty dollars. Francis said, "Gee, thanks, Mister B." And I went right on in. As I entered, I scanned the entire dance floor. I was hoping to find someone with shoulder length blond hair, when I started chuckling. What was I thinking? Nothing is ever that easy. Ninety percent of the people, men and women, had long hair.

I approached the bar, ordered a Singapore Sling and leaned against the rail facing the crowd. I became totally amused, watching people trying to get acquainted with one another. Maybe that's why I enjoyed my job as I do. I'm always amused with others and how they operate.

About a half hour had passed, when through the corner of my eye, some distance away, I saw Lieutenant Bill Rockwell. "What the hell?" I blurted. But the music was so loud, and no one heard. "What the hell was he doing here without his wife?" I wondered. Without being detected, I continued watching. I started thinking back to all the times that I had invited him to Pete's Pub for a drink, and his excuse was the children, when in fact, he had an acquaintance. It was sort of the same type of thing that I was seeking, but. I had an excuse, I was separated for ten years.

They stayed for a while, then shortly after they left, I went back to my Singapore Sling.

After some time of dancing with each lady on either side of me and chatting with the bartender, my quest for romance had diminished. My exciting night out was smothered by the possibility that one of these characters owned the truck outside. Anyone of these people could be the person I was in search of.

I arose from my stool and bid goodnight to the ladies. Then Andy, the bartender said, "See you next time, Mister B."

"Yeah, see ya, Andy," I replied.

I was about twenty feet from the entrance and I could see Frank holding the door open, when suddenly, this blond woman roughly in her mid-thirties, and about 5'6" entered the club. I was completely engulfed, as she entered the "Wildfire". To me, she entered the club in slow motion, she moved like a model strutting down a fashion ramp runway, modeling clothing. She had these electric eyes and a perfume scent that I couldn't ignore. I lost my cool, as she continued walking passed. She no doubt had my attention.

"I turned and followed her to the bar totally mesmerized, was it the Singapore slings?" I wondered. Gosh, she was beautiful. Not the typical mini-skirt, or the see through blouse, or the tattoo around the ankle, that many women find attractive today. No, this woman had class, a lot like Marie's type of class.

She sat on the stool facing forward, looking at the bottles, watching the reflection of others in the mirror. She crossed her legs when Andy the bartender approached and asked, "Would you like a drink, Rita?" Knowing I'd hear every word. "Perhaps he had her as a regular," I wondered. But it was the first time I had ever seen her.

"Yes please, Andy, a Margarita," she replied, as I sat two stools over, on her right.

Rita was wearing black high heeled shoes, with black nylon stockings. Her skirt was shiny, a dark navy blue or black velvet fabric material. It was difficult to determine, with the lighting in the club. The top matched, with just a touch of white blouse peeking over the cleavage area. For jewelry, she had a glimpse of gold above the fringed white blouse. An antique necklace, which matched her gold Bulova watch on her left wrist, and several white gold bracelets on the right wrist.

Rita then turned and looked at me. I couldn't help but notice her glittering diamond earrings and her brilliant blue eyes. Yes, Rita certainly had my attention. She dressed expensively and knowing she sipped Margarita's told me, she showed real class. Just like Marie, both Marie and Rita must have gone to the same school of proper dress, because it certainly showed.

"Wow! What a woman!" I thought.

Angelo A. Fazio

Chapter VIII

Andy returned with her drink, placed it on the bar counter, then turned and asked me, "The usual, Mister B?"

"Yes please, Andy," I replied.

Some time had passed, when during her second drink I heard, "That bastard," Rita muttered. "That son of a b..." she continued. Then took another sip of the Margarita.

"Whoa, whoa," I started speaking. "Rita," I blurted, feeling a little tipsy from the Singapore Slings. "What did the sumbitch, or was his name, bastard? What did he do?"

She turned, looked at me with a smirk and said, "Shut up and drink, bug off."

"Holy Crap!" I thought. "Is this Marie with a blond wig? She looked a lot like her."

I went on to say, "I'm sorry, I couldn't help but overhear your name from Andy. Rita, was it?" I asked. "Rita, the person you're involved with, is it bitch or bastard?"

Rita turned again, sighed, then smiled, shook her head slowly, from side to side and said, "You men, you men are all alike. Weren't you the guy leaving the club, as I was entering?"

"Yes," I said.

"Then why is it you're still here?" she asked.

"Come on Rita, you're the reason why I came back. Stop avoiding the question. What did the bastard hole do?"

She smiled again and said, "The bastard hole? Don't you mean, what did the arsehole do?"

"Alright, alright," I said, "What did the arsehole do? What are you, an English teacher or something?" I chuckled.

Rita exclaimed, "I caught my husband in bed with another woman." She then took another sip of her Margarita.

Then I continued, as she sipped, "How could that bastard, cheat on someone as pretty as you? He must be a real bastard arsehole.

She nearly choked on her drink. "Bastard arsehole," she said. She smiled again and said, "My name is Rita, Rita Hayes."

"Hi Rita, I'm Alec Black. You know, Rita, you obviously noticed me, as I did you, when we passed at the door."

Again she looked at me and said, "Oh, shut up, Alec" with a smile.

"May I buy you another drink?"

"Sure Alec," she said. "The way I feel tonight, you can buy me several." Then she went on to say, "Tomorrow, I swear I'm getting an attorney, it's not the first time I've caught him cheating on me, you know. This must have made the sixth time I've actually seen him with another woman. Who knows how many years this has been going on?"

Instead of drinking the night away at the bar, we danced, then chatted at one of the tables. Getting sloshed was, I'm sure her intentions when she arrived at the Wildfire. However, I was instilling confidence in her, with my own confidence, which was my intention. We talked and laughed, and every now and then, we'd dance to a slow, romantic number, that the DJ would play.

Several hours had passed, as we danced. I lightly held her waist in the palm of my hand, feeling the rhythm, as we kept time with the tempo of the music. The rotating ball, in the center of the dance floor, reflected through her blond hair, leaving me breathless. We danced meaningfully, cheek to cheek. The heavenly fragrance of her perfume lingered round, as we caressed and kissed tenderly, on the dance floor. Our bodies were now shuffling, with the pulse of soft music off in the distance.

Her eyes were shut, as I gazed upon her mesmerizing radiance. And as her eyelids slowly opened her pretty blue eyes reflected the glimmering dance globe high above our heads. Bolts of electricity were felt going through my spine, as I held her close. I was definitely melting into liquid, when I realized, I really hadn't done much drinking at all. Whatever I was feeling, it wasn't created by drinking. That's for sure.

We continued dancing, holding each other, as couples do, late into the night. Then I suggested I'd drive her home. I asked Francis, "Please bring my car right by the door?"

Francis replied, "You got it, Mister Black." Then went off.

I helped Rita with her coat and walked her to the door. My heart was still aflutter. As I was certainly moved by Rita's charm. I assisted her into my car, then we drove off, continuing conversation, laughing, and smiling, as we reached Rita's place.

When we entered her beautiful home, I poured Rita and myself another drink. She placed a soft rhythm CD into the entertainment center, setting the volume just so. Then lit the fireplace, and at the same time asked for her drink. She dimmed the lamps to a glow, leaving just a flicker of flames from the fireplace for atmosphere in the air. No doubt, achieving the mood once set at the Wildfire. Several hours had passed. As we continued dancing and caressing each other firmly, with the speakers of the stereo pulsating a thumping tempo.

To me, Rita was very appealing. Just merely holding her in my arms felt so good, a feeling long lost and forgotten. She had no idea how she made me feel, I started quivering deep within. We tenderly kissed as I held her close and gently leaned her back, cradling her head onto the soft cushion of the couch. I removed her shoes, as she did something with her undergarment. My hands began trembling as I started combing her hair with my fingers and speaking tender words of love into her ear. There was no use, no way out. I was completely captured in loves warm romance and was suspended with excitement, eager to please Rita. I couldn't help myself even if I wanted. I fell deeper and deeper into cherishing the moment, whispering sounds of love lyrics from the music, which kept calling, I caressed her dearly admitting my loneliness to myself.

The roaring fireplace, flaming, looked as I had felt, flaming with passion and desire. Sometime after, Rita fell asleep in my arms, as I held her body close to mine. I could feel her breathing so peacefully, in total contentment.

I shifted Rita over lightly as she slept soundly on the couch, I covered her gently with a blanket not to wake her. Then flipped the glowing dim lamps off, leaving only the shimmering luster of the nearly burnt logs in the fireplace. I slipped my number in her handbag, in the event she wanted to have my number. Then I kissed her long and tenderly goodnight, then locked the door, as I left.

Angelo A. Fazio

Chapter IX

At 5:00am, wandering around like a stray dog, I found myself walking into Mikes Diner, ready for some breakfast.

"Good morning, Mike," I said.

"What brings you in so early on Friday?" he asked.

"I've been on a stake-out all night," I replied. Yeah sure, like I was about to mention I was with Rita, to the "town crier". Not!

"What can I get you Alec? How 'bout two eggs and toast?" as he wrote E.T. on the slip. Mike then clipped the receipt on the rotating lazy susan, above the long window opening, that divided the public counter area to the back kitchen. Suddenly, I heard his wife, Mary, shouting very loudly, "E.T., coming right up." She was an excellent cook, people flocked from all over because of her. Mike was just the in between.

With a regular tone, Mike asked, "Would you like a coffee with that, Alec?"

"Just cream, no sugar," I answered. The Diner at 5:00 am, to my surprise, was very occupied. "A lot of senior citizens apparently get up very early. Perhaps when one hits a certain age, you don't need as much sleep?" I wondered. Whether lack of sleep or too much bed, not enough sleep, this was the place to be. Where sleepy heads wake up to Mary's loud rhythm and very fine breakfast foods.

I sat waiting for my breakfast and pondered, "Today many of the puzzling questions were going to be answered." And I started sorting evidence, in my mind.

Mary knew just how I loved my eggs. She shouted, "Mister B, coming up." Mike reached for the plate that Mary prepared, removing the platter from the kitchen window shelf. "There you go," he said, and refilled my half cup of coffee.

"Perfect, Mike, nice and runny," I said. "I love dunking my toast in the runny egg yokes."

"Gotta keep you coming back," he said.

"No problem," I replied. "Mary keeps cooking like this, I'll never leave. I'll always come back."

It was getting close to 6:00 am. I was wondering if I'd be able to get Bill at home on the phone, so I gave him a ring. After four rings, Maureen, his wife, answered. "H-e-1-l-o? Who is it?" Shoot, I was hoping Bill would answer, just so I could bust his chops from last night at the wildfire. Out with another woman.

"I'm sorry, Maureen, is Bill there?"

"Yes," she said, "but he's sleeping, he had a hard night at the office."

"Maureen," I said, "nudge him and tell him I've got real important stuff to go over with him, in about 30 minutes."

"Alec, right?" she asked.

"Yup, you got it, Maureen." Then I hung up. I figured if I was up all night, then he could do it too.

I gathered the scraped blood samples that I had collected last night at the Wildfire and the registration numbers from the truck. I placed them on the passenger side seat of my hot rod, and I took off. I picked up Bill at his house, and I explained the situation and what he missed viewing on the video. Then proceeded to the Police station, to retrieve the registration ownership's name. Once Bill submitted the plate numbers, it would only be a matter of time before we got a name and residence.

We arrived at the station and after entering the registration numbers, we brought the blood samples that I had collected from the Wildfire night clubs truck, to Trevor at the Lab. It wasn't quite 7:00 am, that's when Trevor arrives, so Bill decided to wait for Trevor, while I went off. Bill wanted Trevor to jump on the new evidence, right away.

As I went on my way, I asked Bill to please phone Marie and I, at the office, prior to going over to the address, when he got it. And that I'd appreciate it. "Whoever the owner of the truck is, he's a possible suspect for an alleged murder. And Marie and I wanna be there," I said.

It was 8:45 am, when I reached the office. I had our little bag of treats, the paper, and a little something special for Marie. I was striving to have some information, before meeting Marie at the office at 9:00. Marie had an excellent mind for sorting things out. "I think women are more capable of handling several topics at once," I thought. "It must be a woman thing."

Right at 8:57 am sharp, the door opened, and Marie walked in. "Good morning, Marie," I said, as she shut the door behind her.

"Good morning, Alec." As a great detective, she noticed the mini sweetheart red roses right off. "Who they from?" she asked.

I replied, "I didn't see a card either, Marie. They were just sitting by the door this morning, as I entered. You must have a special admirer."

She sighed and said, "Ooooooh, Jimmmmmy. He must have sent me flowers. To think I called him an inconsiderate jerk." Marie smiled as she smelled the mini rose flowers. Then looked at me in a peculiar manner. "How do you do that, Alec?" she asked.

"What?" I replied.

"I've come through that door everyday, for the last twenty-two years and each day you look at me, as if it's the first time you've seen me. What's with you, Alf?"

"Oh, I don't know Marie. You're sumthin' special, I guess. After the shooting, I realize it more now than ever before." I looked back at her, the same way she looked at me and said, with my arm and bag extended, "Would you like a croissant?" I then told Marie about the truck in the parking lot and everything that happened last evening, with the exception, of Rita.

Marie had just finished reading the morning paper, when the phone rang. I was still with several pages left, when Marie answered the phone.

Chapter X

"Good morning," I said answering the phone. "Black and Quilby Detective Agency. Marie speaking, How may we help you? Yes Bill, um, yeah, I'll tell him."

Alec asked, "Was that Bill, about going to an address?"

"Yes" I replied, "some guy by the name of Richard O'Leahy was the driver of the plate numbers that you gave to Bill."

"Want to use my car?" I asked, or your truck Alec?"

We decided to drive off in my Viper, as I started thinking about the jerk that shot me. I kept thinking, payback. I looked over at Alec, wondering what was going on in his mind. He usually doesn't say much, but I know his mind is always working. At times, I feel I can read what he's thinking. He always says things that make sense logically. That's one thing I find very appealing about Alec. He's very bright even though he leads people to think he's not.

Just as I was thinking all that, I saw the bulge, from under his overcoat. He was wearing his 38: revolver. Alec doesn't like weapons, from what he's mentioned in the past. Yet, I knew that he knew how to use them, and in fact, very well. He plays like, he doesn't know much about guns, but believe me, I know that he knows!

In the Service, a few of his remaining buddies, have told me he was in "Special Forces", some special military division. They had a special name for him.

They called him "The Mole" from the rodent family "Ground Mole". With real vegetation sticking out of his camouflage assault clothing, he was in a class with only one other. Alec was in a helicopter, most of the time, being shot at, while covering fire. His service buddies told me he received the "Army Service Cross" and the "Distinguished Service Medal" for no regard of his own life, saving others.

The two "Moles" had only received special missions, which meant "Top Secret". Orders only direct from Colonel Davenport who got orders from higher up.

David, the other mole, and Alec usually were inseparable during missions. Once on the ground, both were completely undetectable, when pursuing the objective targets. Alec could be just inches away from the enemy and they wouldn't even know he was there.

When he lost his best friend, he changed. They say he never got over it. The other "Ground Mole", named Dave, shielded Alec's life with his own. Alec has always felt guilty for breathing since that dreadful day. That bullet was meant for him, not David. Since the service, Alec never carries a gun, unless of course it is absolutely necessary and only pulls it out to fire it. "Why would he be carrying one today?" I wondered.

As we came around the corner, I could see Bill and many of the Precinct Officers in full aggressive gear.

"Marie," Alec said, "maybe we should park back a ways, not to get any bullet holes in your new Viper, in case of gunfire. What do ya think?"

Needless to say, "Good idea!" I said.

The bloody truck that Alec spoke about was right out front at the curb of the apartment dwelling. Bill, who was with five of his people, went up the two flights of stairs with Alec and I following at the rear of the group.

Bill knocked on the door. Then knocked again. No answer. He then knocked again and said, "Open up! This is the Police, open up!"

Bill then shouted, "This is the police! Open up or we'll break it down!!"

There was still no answer. With a warrant in hand, Bill instructed his men, "Alright, break the door."

It took one ram and the door went down with such ease, only to find Richard O'Leahy lying on the living room floor with a bullet hole smack center, between the eyes.

"Oh, Crap!" Bill said, as he entered the room. "The man is dead! There goes our lead."

Alec and I approached the scene. Clearly beyond any doubt, even from a few feet away, I recognized him right away. I said, "That's him, that's the jerk, that's the guy that shot me, Bill!"

Lieutenant Rockwell and the homicide department then roped off the area and started collecting further evidence. Alec and I looked around trying to absorb as much of the crime scene as possible, before Bill would ask us to leave.

There, over in the corner, stood Alec, directly staring down over the coffee table. Right on top of the table were two video cameras which were opened without any video cassette tapes inside. Some puzzle pieces were now starting to come together. Yet, Alec and I knew there was something much more here, much more than what met our eyes. Just by looking at the way the body was lying dead on the living room floor told me that he was taken completely by surprise.

"What's on your mind, Alec?" I asked.

"Marie, if you're asking me if this Richard O'Leahy guy knew who shot him, my answer would be, yes. Was he expecting this person that he knew to shoot him? No."

"Do you think he knew too much?" I asked.

"Way, way too much, Marie," Mr. B went on, "especially if someone introduced him to a slug of lead. Marie, what do ya say we split for a while? I can't think clearly with Homicide muttering in the background. Perhaps we could get a cup of coffee or a soft drink?"

"I'm with you," I replied. "There's something I feel I must ask you though, Alec."

"What's that, Marie?"

"It's the dead deer you saw on the video, isn't it. You know, on the back of the pickup truck? The video your son, Fuz, had at the original crime scene, where all this started?"

"You got it, Marie. That's why we're partners. Something just isn't right," Alec said. "Listen, Marie, if my theory is correct, please watch your back no matter where you go, even at the grocery store."

"Why would Alec say something like that? What's he thinking? Am I too close to what's going on?" I wondered. Usually I'm abreast, or a half step ahead of Mr. B, or at least I'd like to think so. It was getting close to lunch, so I suggested Chinese food, I knew a nice little place directly in the center of Exeter, where the food really tastes good. I suggested that we go there instead of going for coffee at the coffee shop near by.

We conversed about how important the video tapes were for someone to actually kill for it. First, I got shot and was left for dead, and now Richard O'Leahy is dead. Everyone in possession of the video, or knowledge of it, gets killed.

After we finished lunch, Alec and I went to the lab to see Trevor.

"Trevor, my man," Alec said. "Whazzzzup?"

Trevor replied, "What gives, Bro?"

I interrupted and said, "Trevor gives! What do you have for us Trevor?"

"Nothing," he said.

"What do you mean, nothing?! You're supposed to have all kinds of information, according to the lieutenant."

"Yeah, I know," Trevor said, "but the Lieutenant wants to see it first."

"The Lieutenant, my butt! We brought the evidence in. We should have first dibs at it. Besides, Trevor, I'm the person who was shot, remember?"

Trevor swallowed hard, then went on to say, "The blood samples that Alec brought in, from the wildfire's parking lot, had four strands of DNA. Two strands were animal and two were human. I matched only two strands from my previous samples. One was animal and the other, was the saliva you gave me, Tuesday.

After almost two hours at the Lab, looking into microscopes and talking with Trevor, we tried to make sense of what was before us at the Lab. We then left for the gas station variety store once again. As we drove down the road, I couldn't help but notice a red corvette following us from three cars behind.

"Alec," I said, "we have a tail."

"Yes," he said, "each time you change lanes, or take a corner, your right rear radius mirror reveals the red car."

"Shall we lose him?" I suggested.

"Why don't we wait, Marie? As much as I'd love to see what your Viper can do, I think being cool about the tail, may give us the upper hand. I still didn't get a good look at the passenger of the pickup truck at the fuel station. Remember on the video? I'm sure Richard O'leahy was the person fueling the truck that night, because owners usually fuel their own vehicles. The guy with long hair, sitting in the truck passenger side, may be this "Palooka" following us. We're looking for that fella as well," Alec said.

As we were being followed, we continued piecing together the crime pieces. "Another strand of DNA," I thought. Three puzzling questions now had answers. Our conversation became involved, as Alec continued,

"Lets not rule out drug traffic," Alec said. "Even though there's evidence towards premeditating murder for profit, there's something missing. I can't put my finger on it. But, we mustn't dismiss drugs. Help me, Marie. You definitely know something, but don't realize it and you may lose your life because of it. I need you, Marie. You're my partner. Think, think!" Alec said.

That's what he always says when he's stuck, without answers, Think, think! What did I know? All I did was remove two video security cameras. I have nothing, and knew nothing of what these criminals wanted.

We got to the service station and I pulled up to pump number seven. I got out and started fueling the Viper. We made it a boycott, only to see where the red Corvette would go. While Alec went into the little convenience store, the red Corvette went right into the same parking lot, where I removed the two security cameras. The driver had long, shoulder-length blond hair. I couldn't make out the plate number, but this may have been the person in the truck that Alec had mentioned. He fit the description.

"Marie," Alec said, after he came out of the store and approached the car, "I went into the store so I could look out through the windows. I used my nonchalant method of checking things out without being noticed. I managed to get the plate number, 'No problem'."

I then said "Are all people in New England that foolish about making major mistakes?"

"By the way, it's not a he," Alec commented, "It's a she in the Corvette. I still couldn't make out the face, but I made out other various features. It's definitely a woman. But, why is there always something obstructing my view? Nothing ever comes easy for me."

We now had the plate number, and a brief description of an individual. What more did we need for identification?

"Alec, what did we come here for?" I asked.

"I wanted to find out if there was an earlier video tape. Maybe from earlier during the day, aimed directly on the fuel pumps."

"Well, was there another camera?" I asked.

"No," he said. "But I'm sure the two video cameras you got from the adjacent parking lot does. There has got to be incriminating footage in them."

I thought for a moment and said, "Bill said that he picked up a bloody shoe print from under a layer of ice, remember? What do you say we go and see Lieutenant Rockwell, then we'll knock off for the day? I'm getting kinda tired, Alec."

"I can see why, Marie! You're like that bunny that never stops. You're constantly on the go even though you've been shot in the chest you're still putting in eight to ten hours a day!"

Alec's funny remark about "Like that bunny" miraculously dispelled my anguish. My tension and discomfort flowed from my body, and I got another jolt of vigor.

Chapter XI

We took off from the gas station and the Corvette once again started following us. The 'Vette, this time, had two cars between us, instead of the three she had before.

"Alec and I now had her license plate number, why was I traveling ten miles below the speed limit?" I thought. I looked over at Alec and without saying a word, I punched the pedal to the floor. Wow! The thrust of the Viper kept me fixed to the seat. What power! I didn't dare look over to see what Alec was doing, in fear I may lose control of the car. The Viper started fish tailing, as both rear wheels were screeching.

Alf must have known what the Viper was capable of doing, because I could hear him laughing, as I clutched the steering wheel for dear life. I was now in my element. I've always had a need for speed, as far back as I can remember. Perhaps it was because of my German Grandfather and his urge to go fast. Presently, my Viper was filling my thirst for zooming. "What a ride!" I shouted. Imagine what Alec's V-12 engine would do, with several hundred more cubic inches and Horse Power, under the hood.

The Corvette that was following, was nowhere in sight. Either she got tied up in traffic congestion, or she wasn't able to keep up. But who cared? I just loved speed.

It wasn't far to the police station. "Thank goodness," I thought, "because I'd probably have a speeding ticket, if it were much further."

We entered the police station and went up to Steve behind the caged counter. When we entered without delay, Steve paged Lieutenant Bill Rockwell. Shortly after Steve's announcement of our arrival, I heard The Lieutenant say over the telephone intercom, "Have them come right in."

Alec knocked on the door. "Come in Guys. Please sit. Would you like a cup of coffee?" The Lieutenant asked, as he turned and filled a cup for himself.

"No, thanks," Alec replied.

"Yes please, Bill," I said. Maybe the coffee will keep me going for a while longer. We then gave Bill the registration number of the Corvette.

Then Alec asked, "Bill, why don't we have another look at the video again? With all the traffic going in and out of the gas station all day long, I think it may show us something."

"What are you looking for?" Bill asked.

"Well," Alec said, "I know I saw a deer on the back of the pickup truck, so that accounts for one animal. Was there another that I missed Bill? We need another animal to account for the second strand of animal DNA."

"So you think there's an earlier vehicle with some other animal?" Bill asked.

"Maybe, or the same truck, different time, or a time in between Monday evening and Thursday night.

That's when I gathered the samples of blood, at the Wildfire night club."

"Yeah," Bill murmured. "You might have something there, Alec."

"That makes sense," I said. "Bill, did Trevor determine the type of animal from the blood samples collected?"

"No," Bill answered, "but Matthews did. He's one of Trevor's assistants working in the lab."

"Well, what did Matt say?"

"Matt said that it belonged to the horse family."

Bill then led us to the video room where we once again viewed the film from the gas station.

"Funny," Bill then said to Alec, "I missed the truck on the first viewing of this very tape. Good eye, Alec."

As the three of us watched the film, there was only one thing of value. Alec brought out the fact, that the blood footprint under the ice was perhaps the same person, Richard O'Leahy, seeing he had the bloody deer on the back of his truck.

After viewing the tape for about an hour, Bill opened the door for us to exit from the screening room. When we heard a young police officer cry, "Lieutenant, Lieutenant!" Here you go lieutenant, as he approached, waving paperwork in front of him. "Lieutenant, here's the registration address of the Corvette you that you requested. Sorry it took so long, the computers were down for a while."

"Thank you, Tim," Bill uttered.

When Bill vocally came out with the name, "Mrs. Rita Hayes", Alec was taken by surprise and said,

"What?! Are you sure? No way, there's gotta be a mistake."

"No Sir, no mistake," Tim the young police officer said. "We double check each time we search, so we don't get accused for false arrest. So, there's no mistake Mister Black."

"Rita, Rita," Alec said in a confused tone.

As our day drew to a close I asked Alec, "Are you okay?"

"Yeah, Marie, I'm okay. Just a real bummer. Ya think you know some people, when in reality, one has absolutely no idea."

"Would you like to go someplace and talk?" I asked.

"What are you suggesting, Marie? Pete's Pub?" Alec asked. "No Marie, you must be exhausted, I'll be fine." And we drove off.

I dropped Alec off at the office, when he kissed me on the cheek, and said, "Marie, would you like me to follow you home?"

"No," I replied, "I'm tired but I can handle it. I'll be fine."

"Okay, then. Get some rest, Marie, and please lock your doors."

I left Alec at the office and drove towards my home, struggling to keep my eyes open. When I arrived at home, I listened to the two messages on the answering machine. Jimmy had called twice, asking if we could do something tonight. But I was so tired, I chose not to call him back. I locked the doors and lied on the livingroom couch, relaxing my aching muscles, and within just a few minutes, I fell right to sleep.

Angelo A. Fazio

FOOLS IN NEW ENGLAND

Chapter XII

Marie dropped me off by the office, instead of going right home.

My son, Fuz, was again now on duty. So I decided, once again, to check out the apartment where Richard O'Leahy was terminated. This time, without the pressure from Bill asking us to leave. I went over to try to satisfy my curiosity.

Richard's bloody truck that was at the front of the apartment earlier was now no longer by the curb. I surmised, if I needed to find it, I'm sure it would be found impounded at the Precinct storage area. But at this time, I didn't feel it necessary. I was interested in just the video cassette tapes.

"Hey, Dad," Fuz said. "What brings you here?"

"First and foremost, to see you," I said. "You're my number one son and I enjoy your company."

"Yeah, yeah right," Fuz said. "What brings you here?"

"Hey, go easy on me son. I misjudged Rita. I thought it was going to be a close friendship. But, forget about it. Surely you know what that feels like. Anyway, son, I need to cross the crime line."

"Why's that?" Fuz asked.

"I'm looking for video cassette tapes. Have you seen any?"

"Oh, the open video cameras," he replied.

71

"Yes, son, the cameras that were on the coffee table." He then went over to check the evidence log, and found nothing.

"What are you thinking, Dad?"

"I was wondering two things, Fuz. One, where are the cassettes tapes from the video cameras? And two, was Richard O'leahy shot immediately after the shooter entered the room, or was the shooter at his place for a while, before he was shot? Those two questions keep bugging me. Do you mind if I just look around?" I asked.

"Yes, I mind," Fuz said. "If anyone gets word of this, it could mean my job."

"Is that a yes, son?" I asked.

"Just don't touch anything, Dad," he whined.

As I entered the apartment, the corpse on the living room floor had been removed. I also noticed the entire place had been dusted for prints. Slowly, I scanned the rooms with urges of wanting to touch. "Screw this!" I thought, and pulled out my gloves placing them on. I started opening things, hoping to find copies of the original tapes, or anything relating to them. Looking into places where you see detectives search, like on TV. Under the sinks, under the drawers, in the toilet holding tanks, upon the ceiling lights, all the places that average detectives commonly look. But of course, I wasn't the average or common detective, and I didn't believe in everything I saw or heard.

There was nothing in the apartment, but as I continued to scan, I saw something peculiar outside on the fire escape. I noticed a flower plant pot, empty, with a little spade sticking out of the frozen soil. "What's this?" I wondered. "Could this have been inside the apartment with plants, and then placed without plants outside, on the fire escape?"

Why would a person go through the trouble of placing fresh potting soil into a flower pot and then leave it outside during these cold winter months? Why didn't he leave it inside after placing the fresh soil? Maybe, just maybe, the plant pot was inside, with a living plant or plants. It certainly was big enough to hold more than just one plant at a time.

I then started looking in the trash containers in each and every room throughout the apartment. Nothing appeared. I was expecting old or new flowers, for that matter, any type of plant or plants.

I then ran downstairs to the big dumpster. I raised the lid and BINGO! My theory was correct and right on. For some reason, the live indoor domestic plants were in the trash. This led me to believe Richard O'leahy, hid the tapes in the pot, and was possibly asking for some ransom. Then again, it was just a gut feeling, but I had to check it out anyway.

I went back upstairs to see Fuz, who was stationed at the door, and explained to him what my theory was. I also mentioned that if I was correct, maybe he could let me view the video tapes first. Then I would put them back where I found them, and let him take the credit for finding the new evidence.

"No, no," Fuz said. "Just leave them out. I'll have to dig them back up again anyway."

My son then helped me bring the pot into the room and after about a half hour had passed, we tried the spade to loosen the soil. The frozen soil needed a little more time thawing, so while we waited, we talked about the case.

After a short while, "BAM"! Buried below the surface of the soil were the two video cassette tapes, wrapped in plastic zipping storage bags. This was a major break through in the case, and I was anxious to share this with Marie. We carefully opened the bags and took out each tape, using our gloves. We then ran the videos on the television, directly located in the same room. Fuz and I now knew more about the incriminating evidence. Not directly pointing a finger, but enough to figure out certain things.

After we viewed both tapes, I wrapped them back into the zipping storage bags, then bid Fuz a goodnight. From there, I left for home.

Friday was usually a good night for television. But, after being up all night, I was very tired. I didn't even bother changing. I removed my boots, set the alarm, and went right to bed.

Chapter XIII

"DING DONG, DING DONG, DING DONG!!" the front door bell rang. I clumsily got up from bed. "Who in the world is at the door?" I muttered with irritation, as I looked at the time.

"11:00AM! Holy Crap!" I said aloud. I never even heard the alarm go off. "Holy Crap!" I continued.

"DING DONG!" the door continued. Hardly anyone ever comes to my door. I looked out the upstairs side window, but I couldn't see the front steps. "Who the hell is it?" I wondered. I hurriedly went down to open the front door. "DING DONG!"

"Okay! Okay! I'm coming!" I shouted.

Slowly I opened the front door, as the sun glared into my eyes.

"Marie?" I asked, as I squinted. To my surprise, Marie was standing there. I continued opening the door all the way and said, "Good Morning, please come in Marie."

"It's almost afternoon, Alec," she replied. "What's happening? This is the second time you didn't show. I thought you were hurt or something. Then, knowing about your total dismay about Rita, I got very concerned."

"No, I'm fine Marie," I said. "I must have been very tired. I didn't even hear the alarm go off, Marie. I'm sorry," and asked her into the house again. Instead, she went back to her car and got a little brown bag along with the newspapers, then brought it all along with herself into the house.

"Good morning," she said. "I decided to come to your home. I hope you don't mind."

"Why would I mind, Marie? You're my partner," I said, as we walked into the living room by the glass coffee table.

"Well, what's going on?" she asked in her German accent. "When I left you last night, I was a little concerned. You were quite taken back about Rita's involvement."

"No problem," I said. "I worked things out, I'm over her. As a matter of fact, after you left, last night, I went back to the apartment where Richard was shot. I went there to get my mind off of Rita, when I stumbled onto something."

"Yes?" she asked.

"Guess what I found?"

"What?" she said.

"Guess Marie"

"No way, Alec," she replied. "You found the video tapes?"

"Yes, I did! I'll tell you all about it, but first, when I'm in your company, Marie, I'd at least like to smell decent. I gotta take a shower. Not only do I smell awful, from wearing these clothes all night, but I also feel sleepy and groggy."

"Yes," Marie said. "I can see you slept in your clothes, but you don't smell awful, Alec. They say the scent of a sweaty man, is supposed to turn women on, you know."

"Yeah, right," I replied.

"Do what you have got to do, Alf. I'll look around and admire your home. It's the first time I've ever been in it."

"Make yourself at home," I said. "I'll be out, shortly," as I walked into the "Bat Cave," (That's what I call my bathroom.)

I got into the shower, then immediately, jumped right out. I nearly burnt myself because the water was very hot. Marie, apparently started talking as she admired my house. But, I wasn't able to hear a word she said, because of the running water.

As I continued my shower, I could hear her shouting loudly by the door, "I'm going upstairs!"

"Okay!" I shouted back. "No problem!" It was funny, how I didn't feel a bit uncomfortable with her in the house. Obviously, she had gone to the bat cave upstairs. When she washed her hands, I could feel the water getting hotter and hotter. I jumped out of the shower again. "Maybe someday they'll perfect the hot water valves, so no one scalds themselves," I thought.

I shortly finished showering, dried myself down, and made a come back to life. Gee, it felt good. I wrapped a bathrobe around myself and went out to see Marie.

"Feel better, Alf?"

"Yes," I replied.

"Wow, your water is very hot," she said.

"Yeah, I know."

We sat and sipped our coffee and munched on the croissants. Not even touching the morning newspaper,

I explained the progress of last night's events at the apartment.

When I finished bringing her up to date on the events that took place, she asked to see the rest of the house. As we walked through the rooms I couldn't help but notice the sun shining through Marie's hair, as she walked by the windows. The slightly mixed reddish tones in her brown color hair, showed a brilliant angel-like hallo around her pretty face. "She was really sumthin," I thought, as I was momentarily daydreaming.

"What's in this room?" she asked, bringing me back to reality, trying to turn the knob.

"Oh, that's just my junk room," I said. And she then turned and walked back towards the stairs.

"Very nice place, Alec."

I know Marie had wondered to herself, why would I lock a junk room? Usually people just throw stuff in a room, but never lock the door.

"Alec," Marie said, "It's getting towards 1:00 pm. I was up early this morning, and I haven't eaten much. I'm starting to get really hungry. Would you like to go for breakfast or maybe lunch?" Marie asked. "There's this place called 'Brunch's' that serves breakfast and lunch all day. What do you say?"

"That sounds great, Marie," I replied. So, I got dressed and we went off in my truck to the Brunch's restaurant not far from Dover.

Chapter XIV

Brunch restaurants are well known in the New England area. They serve not only a very good breakfast, but an excellent lunch menu as well, for people on the go.

Both Marie and I ordered something light, seeing we had a croissant just a short time ago. She had the chicken stir fry, while I had my sunny side up eggs. Not exactly like Mary's, from the diner, but close enough.

The video tapes, that Marie had collected from the parking lot, had filmed several trucks and cars going in and out. However, the vehicle that caught our eyes was a goose neck animal trailer in tow. We discussed what events had taken place, then tried making sense of it.

Richard O'Leahy, the driver of the bloody pickup truck, fueled earlier during the day. He pulled into the same gas pump, he got out of the truck and filled the same truck's gas tank, which he had also done much later during the day. While fueling the truck, he set the automatic lever on, which was located on the back of the nozzle. Then Richard walked around to open the tailgate of the gooseneck horse trailer.

I told Marie what Fuz and I carefully viewed and what Richard was doing. When Richard opened the tailgate, we both noticed a horse with a broken bloody hind leg, in the very first stall, right by where he entered. He walked into the trailer, not even paying any attention to the injured horse. I wondered, "how many other horses get injured during transportation?"

Anyway, that accounted for the bloody footprint under the ice on the pavement. It was the print that Lieutenant Bill Rockwell found, with the homicide department.

However, all this still didn't account or answer the bloody pickup bed, with two other strands of DNA. Yet, there was enough to get Marie and I thinking about what they do with injured horses.

We went back to the office after lunch and started looking up web sites that covered horses with broken limbs. Both Marie and I were very surprised at the misfortune of these beautiful creatures, and the neglect horses receive, when traveling from one place to another. The percentage rate of injured horses was very overwhelming and disturbing.

Now when I look at Jimmy Johnson, and his empire of race horses, I really don't have the same admiration I once had, from just a few moments ago, before learning the information from the computer.

Marie and I looked up various slaughter house companies in the general area. Our plan was to back track and try to follow the events that Richard O'Leahy took, along with his pickup truck.

By phone, the few companies in this general area had never done business with Richard O'Leahy. So, after finding information on the computer, we went into a larger radius, covering as far out as Pennsylvania and Western New York. Marie and I were determined to back track everywhere he and his truck had been.

Marie even more so, because she was actually shot by this dead Banana.

The weather forecast predicted heavy snowstorms, but not in the areas where we had planned on visiting.

They forecasted snow further west of the country, so we decided we would travel by vehicle and show pictures of Richard O'Leahy and his truck, in the event they didn't recognize the name.

Since we're from the coast of New England, we knew that by traveling inland, the weather may become worse. We also knew how unpredictable weather can be, so we decided to take my truck.

Marie and I went back to my place to collect my emergency gear. We collected stuff like blankets, a flashlight, a sleeping bag, and a few other things that would be helpful, in the event we got stranded in the wilderness.

Marie parked her Viper in my garage, where I normally parked my truck. Then we continued on to Marie's place. After we arrived and entered her home, Marie started gathering some things that she thought she'd need. Then she said, "Alf, I'd like to take a quick shower." She didn't know how long we would be traveling and she didn't know when she would be able to shower again.

"Go for it," I said. So she went into the bathroom to shower.

While Marie went into her Bat Cave to shower, I started snooping around, like all good detectives do. She kept a very nice and neatly organized home. Everything was so clean and polished.

As I continued walking through her house, as she did mine, I noticed that her bathroom door was open. I tried not looking, but my nature of interest became difficult to ignore. Heck, the door was wide open, and I saw Marie enter the shower. "Wow! What a fantastic body," I thought. However, being the gentlemen that I am, I politely wandered into another room, and started admiring her collections of various collectibles. She had a locked case of special guns, which no doubt, were apparently brought down from generation to generation. In another room, a collection of stuffed animals and home-made crafts. Obviously showing Marie's gentle feminine side. In another room, a wall of photographs, with her and an instructor in Karate outfits, standing before several achievement trophies. In the same room, off to the left, a glass closet case with Karate belts, all the way up to the final accomplishment, the "Black Belt".

I knew of all her achievements, and participated celebrating each accomplishment, every step of the way. However, as I looked at the glass closet this time, for the very first time, I saw something different. I saw that persistence endured, making her become one of the best. An elite individual, which something very few accomplish.

When Marie came out of the bathroom, I was standing by the livingroom entrance. She came out from around the corner of the bathroom and all she had on was a towel.

"Alf?" she said, while looking at me, straight in the eyes. "Were you peeking at me?" she asked. Without letting me answer, she then said, "I'd be a little disappointed if you didn't Alec."

I smiled and said, "Marie, if we don't get going soon, daylight will be gone and I'll have to spend the night in order to get an early start. You know what I mean?"

Yes, Marie and her appealing accent, 'struck my fancy,' as they say up here. She'd make any man pay attention. But, she's my partner and I always try to keep my behavior under control. Someday though, I fear I'll fail and lose my composure.

Angelo A. Fazio

Chapter XV

Marie glanced at me and saw that I was blushing. She stayed standing there, with just a towel wrapped around her. She knew I really cared for her and she knew that I thought she was sexy.

"Alec," Marie said kiddingly, "is that a banana in your pocket? Or are you happy to see me?"

"No, Marie," I said, "It is this morning's croissant. I stuffed it in my pocket before leaving for Brunch's Restaurant." I realized she knew I was fibbing but I was a very fast thinker. No way could she have thought it was a croissant. To change the subject, I said, "Marie, if we don't get going, it'll be dark and you know it's several hours to get the slaughter houses."

Within ten minutes, Marie was ready to go. She put on layers of clothing, in case it got hot in the truck, or vise versa. Some folks say it's better to layer clothing in the cold weather, instead of just having one coat. From Newington, New Hampshire, we jumped on the highway heading towards New York. We tried the closest slaughter houses first, with no success, even after showing the pictures. So we pushed on.

I talked about going the distance, which was all the way to Pennsylvania, but Marie talked me down and said, "We'll rest." I decided to agree with her, because I was just as happy to spend a night somewhere.

We decided to stay just off the highway, in this little hotel with one bed. Marie slept on the bed, while I slept in the tub. She offered a spot for me on the bed, but I thought it would be best if I didn't. The following morning, we took off at the crack of dawn and went all the way down, west of Hershey, Pennsylvania.

When we arrived at the slaughter house, which we found from one of the computer selections, a big husky guy came out of the office. He was the owner of the company. He reached out his hand and said, "How can I help you? My name is Neal."

I introduced myself, then Marie, and then showed him our identification. After the formalities, we told Neal the reason we were there. Then Neal said, "Come in, come in. You must be exhausted traveling all that way. Please sit down. Would you like something to drink? Please, please sit down." This guy was obviously starving for company. "Feel free to ask, ask whatever you wish. Please, I insist," he said.

Clearly, Neal didn't get many people touring his place. Could it be perhaps because of it being a slaughter house?

Marie and I both had coffees as we talked with Neal. Although Neal was a giant of a man, he was a very pleasant person, helping in every way. One of his arm's muscles, was as big as my thigh! "This guy is huge!" I pondered, "Yet he's as gentle as a lamb." You could tell he didn't enjoy what he did for work. But, as I told him, I'd rather see a man with sympathetic feelings towards animals, than a ruthless insensitive individual having this occupation.

Marie opened her purse and showed Neal a picture of Richard.

"Oh, yes," Neal said. "Why, Mr. O'Leahy, was here earlier during the week. He gave me 1,000 dollars to incinerate one horse. And he gave me a gutted deer to share with the employees. I'd be a fool not to take it.

It was easy money. After he saw the horse going into the incinerator, he left. That was the fastest money I ever made." He went on, "I didn't ask too many questions. I saw a gun tucked in his belt and he looked pretty mean. I didn't want to upset him and wind up in the incinerator, if you get my drift. This Richard character," Neal then asked, "what did he do?"

"We don't know yet," Marie said, "that's the reason why we came all this way. We're trying to figure it out."

"Oh," Neal replied.

Then I had some questions. "Neal, regarding the deer, was it dressed?"

"Yeah, but we call it gutted here."

"How about the horse, was that gutted also?" I asked.

"Yeah, that too. But why do you ask?" Neal replied.

"Just thinking," I said. "Neal, do you think it's possible to put a human corpse in the gutted animal?"

"Well," Neal said, "it's a pretty big cavity, you know. I guess it could be possible, especially if the corpse is in sections. Yes, it could be very possible."

"Thank you, Neal," I said.

We now had been at the plant for almost five hours. I'm sure Neal used this as an excuse to show us the operation. Neal even said a prayer and played music as the departed love ones were being cared for. At around mid-day, Neal took us out to lunch, at one of those Amish all-you-can-eat places, where you eat what you take. After lunch, he also showed us the processes used, along with tons of federal regulations and guidelines the company must use at the plant to ensure air quality in the atmosphere.

As we were getting ready to leave, it was almost as if Neal didn't want us to depart.

We bid our good bye's, and as Marie and I walked to the truck, I said, "Marie, it's just a theory I have, that's all. We can't prove it anyway."

"I understand, Alec," Marie said. "I know what you were thinking, I was thinking upon those very same lines myself. At least we now know that Richard O'leahy was here, and that the trip down wasn't a total waste."

It was getting late again, so we stayed at a local motel for the night. Marie and I felt like we had been on a mini vacation. She seemed to enjoy talking with Neal. He had been a real nice host, and the tour of the factory was very informative. It brought some light on how animals can be taken care of, in a very humane way. We had an excellent experience, even though it was a slaughter house that we visited.

Chapter XVI

The following morning I was up early. Unlike the other motel on the way down where we stayed, this motel had two beds and the rate was around the same. I looked over and saw Marie still asleep. So, instead of disturbing her, I decided to leave the room for a short period of time, while she continued to snooze. I bundled up warmly and went outside to check out the area. The office was located in the middle, and on each side of the office there were ten units. The motel office was open so I went inside. The inside had lots of convenient goods. It had things like coffee, donuts, snacks and soft drinks. All the basic necessities one needs to get motivated in the morning.

I must have spent a half hour, in the office, tinkering with all the little trinkets. I didn't end up buying anything. I just did a lot of window shopping. I then abruptly saw something interesting, as I looked outside the window. A parked glass window replacement truck, reflected a red car at the opposite end of the Motel Inn. I left the office and walked down to get a better look.

"You gotta be kidding!" I said to myself. There it was, right before me. It was the red Corvette, Rita's Corvette. Rita was obviously obsessed, following Marie and I, she must have come all the way from New Hampshire. Marie would be waking up soon, so I then walked back to the office and purchased two coffees, a

couple of donuts and the morning paper. Just as I got to
the door with our morning treats, Marie opened it.

"Did you see me coming?" I asked.

"I heard you leave, you dummy," she responded and
rubbed my head at the same time.

"What have you been doing?"

"Tinkering," I said.

"Tinkering all that time?" Marie asked.

She was teasing me and oh, how I loved it when she
did that.

"Guess what, Marie?"

"What?" she replied, as we started sipping our
coffee.

"We have a visitor on the opposite end of the
Motel."

"Who?" she wondered and asked.

"Red Corvette ring a bell?"

"You must be joking, Alec!"

"No, Marie.   Can you believe it?" I continued,
"Let's enjoy our coffee and donut. She's not going
anywhere. I mean, if she's following and we're not
moving, she'll still be there, right?"

Yes, Rita was definitely following.   I couldn't
imagine anyone driving a Corvette in the winter,
especially when the weather forecaster was predicting
snow.

Marie spoke up and said, "Let's go knock on her
door. What the hell," she continued. "Rita's becoming
a pain in the neck."

"Perhaps you're right, but should we?" Was it really
a good idea?

"Sure, why not, let's do it," I then agreed.

After Marie and I finished our coffee and donut, we dressed warmly, then walked to the opposite end of the Motel. We stopped at the office to pick up a couple more scalding hot, black coffees, just in case we needed them for self defense.

Marie boldly knocked on Rita's Motel room door. "Rita, open up. Come on, open up Rita," Marie knocked again. "Ohhh Riiita," almost like musical notes.

The doorknob started to slowly turn. "That's it, open up, Rita" Marie said. Rita, slowly opened the door the length of the chain. She stood fully clothed with her winter jacket and all. Obviously, she was ready to follow, at whatever time. She must have been just been waiting, as she looked out the six inch length of the chain opening.

"Alec?" Rita said.

"Open up, Rita. Marie and I know you're following us."

"Okay, okay," she said, as she walked outside onto the walkway.

"Why Rita? What role are you playing in this murder?" Marie firmly probed.

"Murder?" Rita reeled. "I didn't kill anyone!"

"No, you didn't," I said. "But, you hired someone to do it for you, didn't you?!"

"No!" she said. "No! I hated the bastard, but I had nothing to do with his murder. Every time I turned around he was screwing around with other women. Ooh, I hated him! I really hated him! But, I would never kill anyone!" Rita went on, "He was involved with a big under world guy hooking people on drugs. Hell, Ralph may have been on drugs himself."

"Ralph your husband?" I asked.

"Yes" Rita replied. "He was never home. I hadn't seen him since Monday."

"WRONG!" I said. "You caught him cheating Thursday night. That's what you said, when we met at the Wildfire."

"Yes," she said, "you're right. I was using you. I used you as an alibi. It was working well, until you started snooping around the horses."

"Wow," Marie said in a soft voice, "that's really got to hurt. I didn't even know you went out with her."

Rita continued, as I listened, "Richard and I were lovers. I'm sorry. Richard worked for the same guy as my husband, Ralph. Neither of them met this under world guy. Richie always got orders by phone. Monday night I was in the truck with Richie, at the gas station. I was really nervous that night. Then Tuesday night, when I saw the police at the same station I couldn't help but notice you and Marie prying around.

I've been watching you two, and the police snooping around. I swear, Alec, I didn't kill him. Richie told me that he got a deal from the big guy. He got a deal that he couldn't refuse. Richie was asked to wipe out my husband Ralph for Fifty Grand. Richie thought, great! He'd get rid of that craphead husband of mine, then run away with me, along with enough money to start a new life." Rita then got teary-eyed. "Mr. Black? I'll tell you whatever you want to know, if you let me go. Please?" She said in desperation, then started to whine, "I haven't even had a cup of coffee yet."

"Marie," I said, "can ya please keep an eye on her, while I get the three of us some more coffee? But, Marie, don't trust her, whatever you do. She's really a fox. Very sly"

While I went to get the coffees, seeing our coffees were now cold, from standing outside, by the doorway, Rita told Marie how she and Ralph should have never gotten married. She had met Ralph while Ralph was trying to get her hooked on drugs. She admitted that Ralph was just a smooth operator. Marie couldn't believe what she was hearing. Rita was right, she should never have married Ralph.

I briskly walked on my way back, carefully juggling the three coffees. Marie noticed that I gave her a coffee first.

"Here you go, Marie," I said.

Then I gave Rita her coffee.

"Why are we standing out here in the freezing cold?" I asked.

Angelo A. Fazio

Chapter XVII

"I don't trust anyone, since Richie was killed. Not even you guys. I don't care if we freeze out here. We're not going in," said Rita.

"Ooookay," Marie said.

Rita continued her side of her story. "Richie told me that he planned to kill Ralph, my husband, while hunting. They kinda new each other from working for the same guy. They planned it and went on a hunting trip. Together, they shot a pretty good sized deer. Richie told me that Ralph even helped him dress the deer out in the wilderness, before Richie killed him. After he killed Ralph, he tried stuffing his body into the deer, but it didn't fit very well. So, he sectioned Ralph up. That was the only way he'd fit. The only problem he said he was concerned about, was that if when he got to the slaughter house to incinerate, the guys would take the venison and discover Ralph's body. So, Ralph's body stayed outside, like in a freezer, until he got a horse from the racing circuit. That was the other job Richie had. He transported horses to the slaughter houses, as well as live stock to surrounding horse farmers. Usually he'd liquidate the horses locally."

"Wait a minute. Time out," I said. "Marie and I asked the local places, and they said they didn't know him even after showing Richard's picture."

"Yeah right," Rita said, "like they're going to tell you who Richie was, what he was doing, and who he worked for. Give me a break!" Rita whined. "Anyway, he finally got a horse in trouble that had to be put down. That's why this one horse was special, because Ralph's body was in it. That's why he went down here, to Pennsylvania, thinking no one would ever track him down, this far out. That is until you two came along."

Marie then blurted out, "Give us a good reason why, why should we believe you Rita?"

"Because, you and I have something in common you and I hav…"

"Fiiiit! Fiiiit!" The sound of rifle fire, with a silencer.

Rita was shot twice, right before our very eyes. Marie darted into the room, as I reached out to catch Rita going down. Rita was shot pretty bad. It was something I've seen so many times before in my past.

"What the heck?" Marie asked with fear in her voice. "Was that meant for me?"

I brought Rita into the room, then called 911, who dispatched an ambulance.

"Alec, what's going on?" Marie asked.

"Marie are you alright?" I asked.

"I'm okay, but I don't understand what's going on?"

"Marie, this was no Bang Bang, you're dead type of shooting. This shooting was a rifle, with what I call a Muffy."

"Yes, so?"

"Think about it, Marie. Why would just anyone go around shooting someone? Especially with a silencer? Rita was the intended target. This could be the under world stuff she was just talking about. I saw no fire flare on the second round of gunfire, which tells me instantly that it was a skilled Rifleman, or a Marksman perhaps."

The direction of impact told Marie and I that the shots were fired from somewhere behind Marie.

"Marie, where I was standing, I would have seen some flash, or even a small tell-tale of smoke. But, I saw nothing, Marie. Absolutely nothing.

"What are you thinking, Alec?"

"This could only mean two things: One, this guy was good at using camouflage during daylight hours, and Two, Rita was the objective target."

Before the police and ambulance arrived, Marie and I applied all our rescue knowledge for Rita. Between my past war rescue encounters, and Marie's Far East pressure point abilities, we stopped the loss of blood and stabilized her vitals. We knew, when the EMT's arrived, Rita had a fighting chance for survival. Though Rita had used me, I was glad she seemed to be surviving the sniper's gunfire.

"Here it was, plain daylight, at 8:30am in the morning, and I wasn't able to even see movement of this sniper. Yeah, he was good, real good," I said.

"First I was shot," Marie said. "Then it was Richard, now Rita, right before our eyes. And Ralph was another, but in a different way. What are we missing, Alec?" Marie asked.

I started to wonder if Jimmy had any place in all this, where horses were involved. "No, no way," I thought.

By the time Marie and I left the motel, heading back to New Hampshire, it was almost 4:30 in the afternoon. Explaining to the police that we had nothing to do with the shooting, took some doing.

Finally after a while, we were back on the road. Snow started accumulating, shortly after we started back. About an hour of driving had passed, and during that time, a good four inches of snow had stuck to the pavement. We knew we were in trouble, especially up here in the Pennsylvania mountains. We needed to find some shelter, but there were very few places to spend the storm. According to the map, the nearest town was about another 40 miles away from where we were. At the rate we were traveling, it would take us at least two hours to get there. I wasn't worried and Marie was doing fine feeling comfortable with me driving. "Of course" I thought, "I am a smooth driver."

We continued on, as the snow increased in depth, and the roadways became impossible to see. The long stretch, on highway 84, outside of Hershey, PA, was being smothered by the damp heavy curtain of snow and fog. It was Mother Nature's wrath.

My tension started to build, as I griped the steering wheel. I was straining to see through the dangerous blizzard conditions of Pennsylvania's snow, which engulfed the car ahead of us. The winking tail lights had been comforting, letting us know there was another human, sharing the evening's raging storm. When suddenly, the car in front surrendered and decided to swerve to the side. Another 10 miles to the next town, could we make it?

We pushed on, when not much farther down the highway, for the first time ever, I admitted the probability of not making it. It was not good news. The rear tires were starting to lose traction, slipping, as we slowly were unable to continue. The fuel tank was three quarters full, we thought at least we would have heat. However, the engine died out after two hours of being still. The cold was now starting to infiltrate into the cab. Thank goodness we didn't take the Viper. There was nothing now to do but battle the freezing temperatures and wait. Wait for a plow, or for some assistance. At the very best, we'd be able to follow behind a plow, into the next town. But for now, at least, we came equipped with all the proper things one needs for survival.

I was in the front seat, while Marie got into the back seat of the huge crew cab pickup.

"Alf?" she said. "You think that sniper guy, who shot Rita, is still out there following us?"

"Yes," I replied. "Most likely, he's out there, but don't worry. Yes, this guy is good at what he does, but not good enough, Marie."

"What do you mean?"

"Whoever this guy is, he reminds me of myself some years back."

That's when I decided to open up and say, "Have you ever heard of me speak of the name David Anderson?"

"Maybe once or twice," she said, not knowing if I had told her, or if one of my Military buddies did.

"Well, Dave was my best friend. I met him in the service. We trained together for whatever Uncle Sam had in mind. If only he had let me take the slug, David may have been alive today. Who knows, maybe I would have survived the wounds of war. All I know is, it's tough, not knowing. He took my bullet. It's something I have had to live with everyday, for the rest of my life." I continued on, "No, Marie, this guy, whoever he is, isn't going to bother us tonight, I'm sure. This weather is for neither man or beast. He won't bother us until we get back, I'm sure."

"My gosh, Alec, I'm starting to shake and it's not from fear."

I tried starting the truck one more time, only wearing the truck battery down. Then went into the rear seat with Marie. I took out my sleeping bag and said, "Marie, get in."

Marie felt definitely warmer in the bag, but it was below zero degrees and she was still shaking.

"Alec," she said, "if I'm in your sleeping bag, shaking, you must be freezing."

"Marie, I only have the one bag," I said.

"Yes, so," she said in her broken German accent "get in here and warm me up." She insisted.

In order to even fit into the bag we had to remove some clothing. Shortly after we entered the bag, I placed my right arm around her mid-section and we both felt this overwhelming closeness to each other. Our body heat started to warm us both and it was then, that Marie stopped shaking. I know that Marie thought maybe I'd try something funny, seeing that we were nearly nude. But, I didn't even try to kiss her. I could tell that she sensed that I was blushing. I couldn't see her face, where she was in front of me, but she could tell. After 22 years, she knew me very well.

Knowing that someone wanted Marie dead, I honestly could tell that she felt very safe, with my arm wrapped around her.

In the early morning hours, Marie awoke and seemed to be feeling a bit uncomfortable. "Alf, Alec, wake up, wake up." As I awakened, she asked, "What's this hard thing against my back?"

"Huh?" I replied very groggy. "Oops, sorry Marie. It must be the flashlight I stuffed in the sleeping bag."

"Yeah, right," she said, as I rolled over and her discomfort went away.

It was about five o'clock in the morning when the first plow came around and tapped on the window.

"You guys okay?" the driver asked, from outside.

"No," I said. "I'll be right out."

I got out of the sleeping bag and the air change was very noticeable. Wow! It was cold! It's amazing how much heat the human body can generate in a very confined area.

"Holy mackerel, what a big flashlight," Marie said as she looked at me and smiled. "Marie, it's a small flashlight, not even an average size."

"Yeah, right," she muttered.

I tried stuffing the flashlight into my pants. But, the flashlight didn't disappear, not until I draped my sweater over the belt line of my trousers. I opened the door and went out for help from the snow plow driver, as Marie got dressed. Then she also came outside to help. The plow driver and I had everything under control within a few minutes.

"Marie, could you please try the engine and start the truck, while I diddle with the engine cables?" I asked.

Marie turned the key on and the engine started right up. We couldn't wait for the engine to warm up. The very first thing she did, was put the heater on, a simple thing, that can mean so very much.

We followed the kind snowplow driver, into the next town. It took a while traveling very slow, because of the plow pushing snow, but, who cared? We stopped for breakfast in the small town. Then continued following the plowed route that the city workers provided, back to the interstate highway.

The views in Pennsylvania with the new falling snow were beautiful, especially up in the high Schuylkill County mountain area. You'd have to see to believe the wondrous breath taking sights, to really capture its brilliance.

As Marie said earlier, this was more like a vacation break than a business trip. As we traveled through each state, you could see the hard earned tax money at work, in the areas where there was substantial snowfall. The interstate snow plows and tractors were busy, desperately trying to bring the major highways back to passable standards. The snow line went through the New Hampshire area, but there was no where as much snow as in the inland states.

Our truck pulled into Exeter center, just before 2:00 pm. We were just in time to catch the "All You Can

Eat" Chinese food buffet. Yummy! It also gave Marie and I a chance to get cleaned up, from sleeping in the truck all night.

Angelo A. Fazio

Chapter XVIII

With Rita now in critical condition, back in Pennsylvania, and the shooter I'm sure was still clipping at our heels every step of the way, we went back to the office after lunch. However nothing in the office was helpful, so we decided to rest and call it another day. We decided to meet back at the office the following morning at nine o'clock.

The four DNA strands were now accounted for. We had the deer strand, the horse, Richard O'Leahy, and Ralph's, Rita's husband. But, who wanted them, including Rita, out of the way, and why?

I've lost track of how many days Alec and I have dedicated to solve this bloody gas pump mystery, all I know is, it started last Monday night. I'm sure it's more than Mr. Black expected.

Just as I decided to get up for a coffee at the perculator the office was fired upon! A bullet came right through the window. If I hadn't turned and leaned forward to stand, I would have gotten shot again.

Both Alec and I hit the floor. Then Alec inquired, "You okay, Marie?"

"No," I said. "Why me? What the hell did I do?"

Alec then said with anger, "Now I'm really pissed! What is it they want, your life? Bull Crap! They can't have it!"

When we felt comfortable to get up from the floor, we again focused harder on all our events, including my past clients and Alec's past, even involving the military.

Any and everything that may be connected to our present murder crimes.

As it turned out, last August, I received a phone call. It was a call regarding a horse farm, Miss Lizabetty's horse farm. The call was from Miss Lizabetty's father. He called our agency for help, but, we chose not to except the client. The reason we gave him, was that it was too far out. It was someplace in the western part of New York.

When things were getting a little slow around the office, I decided to give the old man a jingle. He told me of the problems at his daughter's horse farm, and also added that the problem still existed.

I found out Lizabetty owns the horse farm just outside of Rome, New York. For no apparent reason, her Morgan race horses kept breaking their legs. Their legs were breaking while running in the actual horse races, not every race. But several horses would have their limbs just give out, causing the horse to go down. Some of her horses also broke limbs right at the starting gate.

I had decided to go out to the horse farm to get acquainted with Lizabetty and I got involved with the situation.

"Marie?" Alec asked, "regarding your case with Lizabetty and her horse farm, what did you do that only took your appearance, of eleven days to stop horses from having accidents?"

"I don't know," I said. "When I arrived at her place, within days things started to change. Then, suddenly, during the last couple days, just before my departure from her ranch, the horses stopped breaking their limbs. I was credited for the sudden change, and the firm was paid quite handsomely for our services. I honestly don't see a connection, Alec. Where are you going with this?"

"Marie," Alec asked, "when did you bump into your old dear friend Jimmy?"

"I see now, where you're going," I said.

"Well, when?" Alec asked.

"I bumped into Jimmy coming back from Rome, New York. I was on my way back from the horse farm, heading home, when I stopped for fuel and something to eat. It was just outside Schenectady, right on route 90. To my surprise, Jimmy and I were standing in the same line waiting to order food."

"Did you see him in line or did you see him get in line?" Alec asked.

"What's the difference?" I asked.

"You know," Alec said, "you're just as good as I am at this. Don't you think it's funny, you bumping into Jimmy, way out from Rome, New York, knowing he lives here in New Hampshire? What's the chances of that, Marie?"

"No, I don't think it's strange at all. Jimmy has investors all over the country, and I believe Lizabetty was one of them. Sounds to me like you're grasping at straws, or that you may be a little envious or jealous of Jimmy."

"Perhaps Jimmy was following you," Alec said, trying to be as compassionate as possible. Knowing how Rita had treated him, bragging how she used him, without any compassion.

"I don't think so," I replied.

"Maybe you should give Miss Lizabetty a call in the morning and find out how things are going," said Alec.

"Yes," I replied. "Tomorrow."

"Just don't be surprised if she's dead," Alec said.

"Why would you say that? That's an awful thing to say, Alec."

"Well, Marie," said Alec, "Rita, just before she was shot, was saying you both had something in common. Did you both know Jimmy at one time or another?"

"Oh, come on, Alec, give me a break!"

"All I'm saying, Marie, is, if Lizabetty is dead tomorrow when you call, I see a common denominator. Whom, at my opinion, may have something to do with all this."

"Cut the crapola, Alec. Look elsewhere, 'cause in my opinion, Jimmy is a decent man. Knock it off!" I said.

"No problem," Alec replied. "I'm just touching all bases. When you call Lizabetty tomorrow, I just hope she still is there. Marie, I really don't want Jimmy as the common denominator either. I like Jim."

Chapter XIX

Don't get me wrong, I, myself, think Jimmy's the greatest, but when it comes to shooting my partner Marie, that's where I draw the line. Jimmy is cool, as cool as a cucumber. He's a very wise man, and also filthy rich. Yeah, why would he wanna throw all that away? Maybe Marie is right, maybe I am pulling at straws. I decided to start looking into other areas of possibilities.

Both Ralph and Richard were involved in drugs. They also both knew Rita. Now two are dead and Rita is still in critical condition in Pennsylvania, shot by some unknown sniper. If Lizabetty is dead tomorrow, then we must find the sniper.

Marie called the horse farm out in New York, the following morning, to find Miss Lizabetty alive and well. I was very glad she was alive, but it threw my theory right out the window. Marie and I decided to see what Lieutenant Rockwell had put together, so we called the Lieutenant at the station, to let him know our intentions.

I called Steve, the officer behind the cage counter, on the phone.

"Hey, Steve, can you notify Lieutenant Rockwell that we'll be dropping by in about thirty minutes?"

"Sure," Steve said, "who's this?"

"Tell him Marie and Alec. He'll know who we are."

"You got it, Mr. Black," he said and hung up.

On the way to the police station, Marie wondered about Rita. She started talking about how, under different circumstances, they may have become great friends. Rita had, no doubt, effected Marie as she did me.

Marie asked, "So how long have you been going out with Rita?"

"What do ya mean?" I said.

"You know what I mean Alec. You don't have to be a rocket scientist to figure you and Rita were going out," Marie said. "The reaction on your face the other day when she said she was in love with Richie. Then again, there was your reaction when she said she used you."

"I'm that readable, huh?"

"Yeah," Marie said.

"I'll tell ya the truth Marie. I just met her Thursday night at the "Wildfire club". She and I spent a little time together, that's all."

"It looked to me like a little more than that Alec, especially when we saw Rita get shot, right in front of us," Marie said.

"Okay, okay, Marie, I was concerned for Rita, but Rita just thinks about Rita. She obviously likes using people. She used me. Like that's a great start for a wonderful relationship," I said. "Besides, I'm not over my wife Olga yet," I said.

"What do you mean? It's been ten years now," Marie said.

"Marie, right now, there's only one woman in my life, and that's you. If anything ever happened to you,

I'd be very hurt. I'd fall apart. I'd lose the best friend I've ever had."

"Oh, come on Alec, give Rita a break. Give Rita a phone call tomorrow. See how she's doing," Marie said.

When we arrived at the Police Station, Marie went up to see Steve at the counter, and mentioned that we had just arrived.

I sat on the bench, wondering what Lieutenant Bill thought about the video tapes that my son, had brought in. Marie then sat beside me.

"We must wait a while," Marie said, "Someone's in with the Lieutenant right now."

"Okay," I said, as we sat quietly on the bench for a few minutes waiting to hear Bill call us in. Shortly after, I noticed a young woman came out of the Lieutenant's office. It was the same woman I saw at the Wildfire Club that was sitting with Bill. I saw them together the other night and it looked as if they were drinking beer, and then they left together.

I nodded and smiled, as she walked past us and exited the door. Then Marie and I got up and entered Bill's office.

"Hey, Bill," I said, "have you seen the new evidence? The video cassettes tapes that my son found at the apartment and brought in?"

"What tape?" Bill said. "This is the first I've heard of something new."

"What do ya mean, what tape? The tapes," I said. "My Son, Fuz, called me last night to say that he found two video cassette tapes and he said he was going to bring them in for evidence. That tape!!" I said.

I knew damn well, my son and I viewed the tapes at the apartment together. But I didn't want to get Fuz in trouble by mentioning it.

"Where's Sargent Fuz?" Bill asked the clerk, just outside his office door. Then went on to say, as he walked back to his seat, "If he had new evidence, I'm sure it would be downstairs in the evidence room."

We all went down, to see Sargent Patricia Adams, at the caged door of the evidence room.

"What brings you down here, Lieutenant?" Patricia asked.

"Did Fuz bring any new evidence in last night? We're looking for two video cassette tapes?"

Sargent Patricia brought out the roster log and looked down the list. "Last night, no," she replied, as she turned the roster board for us to view. "No, sir, no evidence was submitted last night at all."

Something was wrong, I thought. My son would never suppress new evidence. My former wife and I taught Fuz the golden rule, "honesty is the best policy".

Marie could tell that I was getting upset when I said, "Bill, when was the last time my son called in? Any record of that?"

"I'd have to check the records log upstairs," Bill said.

I started to feel like I was led along by the hand, as we went up and down checking the log books. We found Sgt. Fuz's last call to the precinct. It was placed at 10:00 pm, two hours before the end of his shift.

Even Marie knew something shady was happening. Since she knew Fuz calls in every hour. It was something I taught him early in his career as a police officer…Just a quick radio check, to make sure things are functioning properly.

Bill hadn't been very helpful. He had nothing to add to the investigation. I then asked Bill to go with us to the apartment where Richie was killed.

"Somewhere in that apartment is a 12" or 14" flower pot. My son told me about it on the phone. We need to check it out Bill. Something isn't settling right!" I exclaimed.

The three of us departed again, this time to the apartment. When we arrived at the apartment, there was a cop on duty by the door.

"Hi, Joe," Bill said. "What do you have?"

Joe replied, "No one has entered since I've been on duty, Sir."

"Thanks, Joe," Bill said.

We entered the room and I knew exactly where the pot was, because of the night before. I couldn't help but notice Bill glaring right at the fire escape, where the pot once was. Then his eyes shifted and continued to scan the room.

"Nothing seems to be disturbed," Bill said. "Oh, that must be the pot that you were talking about, Alec."

We walked over to the soil spilled flower pot.

"Is this where the tapes were?" Bill asked.

"That's where Fuz said they were, Bill," I said.

"Is there anything else you want to look at while we're here?" Bill continued.

I thought for several seconds and wondered where the videos could have gone, then said, "No, the tapes were what I was interested in, and they appear to be gone, so I can't think of anything. How about you, Marie?"

"No, I can't think of anything either."

"Well, I guess that's it then," Bill said. "I've got to get back to the office. Catch you guys later. Keep me abreast on what's going on."

As Alec and I walked to the truck, I could hear Alec muttering, "Where's my son, what the hell happened?!"

Alec drove back to his place not saying much. He was thinking and showing expressions of concern on his face. I could tell he was worried about Fuz. "Was Fuz another victim of the sniper?" I wondered.

When we arrived at Alec's house, the minute he stopped the truck, he got out and hurriedly opened the front door. He went in and went right up the stairs, and I followed.

We reached the top of the stairs, and without saying a word, Alec then reached above the door frame of the junk room and with his fingers he gently shifted along the top and located the key to unlock the door. As he turned the key to unlock the door, he turned the knob slowly and cautiously pushed it open. The room looked as though he hadn't opened it in years, or since the home was built. The dust on the floor, inside the room, must have been a half inch thick. While just over the threshold in the hall, it was as clean as a whistle. There was dust everywhere in the room, with long spider and cobwebs hanging on everything in view. You needed a knife to cut a path to wherever you were going in the room. However, he paid no mind of the webs and just walked right on in, slightly waving his arms in front of him. I looked in amazement.

"This was no junk room, this room was Alec's entire life," I thought. He had photos of himself and family from when he was a kid, up until the time he locked the door. A family that I knew nothing about.

On the walls, there were pictures of his war buddies, along with two framed cases of many medals, including the "The Army Service Cross" and the "Distinguished Service Medal". In the closet were hanging uniforms, and sentimental clothing of his children, and his former wife, Olga. Everywhere you looked there was some part of his life that I had no idea existed.

Alec went directly to this huge, and I mean huge, desk loaded with all kinds of meaningful sentimental Military pictures, picking up one and blowing it off. Suddenly I heard, "YOU SUMMA BITCH!"

"What?" I said.

"Colonel Davenport, that bastard! He must have trained others like David and I." Alec went on, "I kinda knew that when Rita was shot, before our eyes. The two bullets, that were fired, entered her chest nearly on top of each other. I had thought right off, it's the work of an "Elite Rifleman". But I didn't put it together until I saw Bill look at the fire escape."

Alec handed and showed me the picture he blew off. There was a group of four guys dressed in combat uniforms. Now I knew Alec's best friend, David, and what he looked like. He was about the same height as Alec, but not as muscular. He was African-American and they had their arms around each other's shoulders. They were smiling with their thumbs up, looking beyond the person taking the picture. It was like someone telling them to pose properly.

"It was just the two of us, chosen from the entire battalion of troops. The Colonel said there were no others," Alec said.

"But how did all this tie in?" I asked.

"Marie," Alec said, "I'm starting to see the entire picture now, I'll explain."

Chapter XX

Before he explained, Alec said, "Let's go downstairs Marie. This room gives me the creeps. Too many terrible memories and visions of my friends being slaughtered, killed and torn apart, all in the line of duty."

Again, he locked the door and placed the key up above the door frame. Then we went back downstairs to sit by the coffee table.

He then started, "During the Vietnam era, starting in the sixties, there was easy access to many different forms of narcotics. It was quite sickening how fast it spread in all ranks of the military over there. Many of the upper ranks knew the crap that was going on, and in some cases, induced it. Induced, to keep calm among the troops.

Later during the seventies I heard it got worse from guys I knew, who had come out of the bush. But, I can only account for my time frame. It was like instant money for involved upper ranking officers. Once the guys got hooked, let's face it, what else could the troops do with their monthly wages, especially in the bush?

The Colonel came from New England, and I knew of his involvement concerning his 'Circle of Life', as he put it. As a rule, I didn't give a crap about what the others did, or didn't do. Who gave a 'rat's ass'? I figured it was their life, 'Live and let live'. The only times it did bother me though, was when my life depended on their's. Many times I was involved on missions with guys who did use it, and many times I knew my life was in jeopardy. The Colonel nearly always had David and I work on the same missions. However, at times, he involved David and I with others without 'Top Secret Clearance' status. Thinking back, I think it was the Colonel's way to keep David and I in line. Knowing he was able to put us in harm's way at any given time, it kept him in control.

My last mission in 'Nam was with David. That's when David acquired my ticketed cartridge, a slug to the chest. I now see that I was being terminated, erased, for what I knew of the 'Circle of Life'. David saw I was being fired upon and intercepted my execution attempt. After all these years, I now think he was gunned down by one of our own.

When Rita was hit, with the two slugs, almost on top of each other, I figured that an 'Elite Rifleman' was behind it. The whizzing sounds of bullets by our ears brought me right back to the sounds and visions I'm trying so very hard to forget.

Was the underworld Kingpin Colonel Davenport? Rita said that both Ralph and Richard worked for some big unknown drug underworld guy. First Ralph got wiped out from Richard. Then Richard got wiped out by the sniper. Then Rita got hit from the same sniper, or should I say the Colonel's Elite Rifleman. Is my son another victim from this sniper? That's what got me thinking on the way home. What better way to traffic narcotics, pot, or drugs, or coke, or whatever, than in a horse trailer. It doesn't even need to be bagged, going from one state to another. 'For crying out loud' It's grass, it's alfalfa, it's hay and in it's natural state easy to transport.

Marie, picture if you would, drugs being shipped in their natural state. It could look like hay. It could possibly be shipped to livestock, like horses, as their eats! That stuff could be disguised as hay and it could be hanging around a horse farm. No ones the wiser. According to Neal, we know the horses are sometimes gutted, and we also now know about hurt horses and what they do with them."

"Holy mackerel!" I said. "You're making logic Alec. Let's bring this to Lieutenant Rockwell."

"Hold up, Marie," Alec said, "Let's not throw this, we don't want to make an arse of ourselves, especially in front of Bill."

I agreed with Alec then I continued, "Rita said that Richard had two jobs, one was with this underworld person, and the other was driving horses for someone. Maybe Bill can look up in record files, especially criminal records, perhaps Richie has a moving violation record or parking tickets or something Bill may find to be helpful to where Richard O'Leahy worked. I'm sure the police would have no problems finding that little tidbit."

"Sharp thinking Marie," Alec said.

We continued talking for a while longer, then cruised over to the precinct to see Bill once again, from Alec's home. Bill tried filling in some of the blanks as he searched files during conversation. When suddenly Bill came up with a minor vehicle violation. As it turned out, Richard worked for Jimmy Johnson's estate.

Richie worked as a sole drive, directly under the supervision of the senior foreman. According to the records, Richard was stopped for speeding on officer Mike's watch, during the evening hours.

Richard stated to officer Mike the truck he was driving didn't belong to him, but to the Johnson's horse farm. Also that he was employed by the foreman. The foreman's name here on record is named Fred Dimers. Better known as "Freaky" Dimers, as Richard O'Leahy says here. He was the transporting manager for livestock, whether it was alive or dead.

We were putting all the facts together, and everything was going fine at Bill's office, until Alec brought up the Colonel and his "circle of life".

"Colonel Davenport!?" Bill went ballistic. He wasn't buying it, no way did he agree. Bill started swearing profusely at Alec.

"No way, Alec, not the Colonel."

"Well," Alec said, "who the hell else then Bill?"

"I don't know," Bill said, "but it's not the Colonel."

"FINE!" Alec said very angrily. "IT'S NOT THE COLONEL!"

In anger, Alec then said, "THEN FIND MY SON, COP!!" And stormed out of Bill's office, slamming the door.

I watched him leave, then said, "He's been under a lot of stress, Bill." Then I also left his office.

Alec made sense, but was he right? Alec drove us back to his home, again not saying much along the way. When we arrived at his place, I picked up my Viper, which was still parked in the garage, and I said good night. I then started on my way towards my home. Needing to stop once, to pick up some photos and cosmetic needs at the drug store. I thought about Jimmy, as I drove home, and I wondered if he wanted to go out tonight. I wanted very much to tell him about one of his employees. His foreman in particular, Freaky Dimers, and how he was a suspect for murder. I knew Jimmy would help the police, he's helped them so many times in the past, back when I knew Jimmy before.

Chapter XXI

When Marie left, I was determined to put all this crap to rest. I didn't want Marie to think I had flipped out. But, I was certain I knew I wasn't wrong. I was positive my past also had something to do with the murders and all this business with the drugs.

Marie and I cracked the case of Freaky Dimers and his role in the transportation portion of the horse and drug activities. But I wasn't buying the fact that an "Elite Riflemen" wasn't involved with Rita's shooting. When it came to the snipers, I knew it involved my past.

Back then, we were real close. There were the four of us, Colonel Davenport, Bill Rockwell, David Anderson and myself. When the Colonel started his "Circle of Life" organization, that's when Bill, Dave and I backed away. We didn't want to be involved with screwing up other people's lives. We knew it was wrong. It was wrong to make a profit on others, of a weaker mind.

I started thinking about the four of us. David was dead, so he's out of the murder scenario. I knew that the Colonel was the king pin. So who was left? Lieutenant Bill and myself, and I knew where I stood. So that only left Bill Rockwell. What was Bill's role back then in 'Nam? Did he cross over and become the Colonel's comrade?

"What am I thinking?! Should I be questioning Bill's loyalty? Geez, we went through hell together!

He and I go back a long way," I thought. "Bull Pucky! 'Trust no one.' That's what my favorite agent says from the 'Z Files' television program. Yes, I will question Bill's loyalty, especially when he looked directly at the fire escape back at the apartment. And then he made it look as if he was scanning the rest of the rooms. Why would Bill do that? And then say, 'Nothing appears to be disturbed.' He knows that Marie and I are the best detectives in the area. Is he as foolish, as the fools in New England criminals, that Marie and I often speak about?"

My thoughts continued, "And what about my son, what happened to him? Did he call the Lieutenant with the new evidence we found in the flower pot? Did Bill have the sniper erase my son? Or, is Bill himself the sniper? Did Colonel Davenport also have Bill certified as 'Top Secret Terminator Regulator', as David and I called it?"

I couldn't believe I was thinking upon these lines, these lines of internal stupefaction and shocking re-evaluations.

"By gosh!! What am I thinking? What if this is true?" I said to myself. "If so, then I must concur with my gut feeling. Bill and Freaky Dimers are involved with one another! Or could they also be involved with Jimmy? Bill looked up the records, and pointed the finger at Freaky Dimers. Was he shifting the crimes away from Jimmy? Or are the three of them enrolled with one another?"

I mumbled, "Am I getting carried away with myself? Richard and Ralph transported horses around the country and also at the same time, causing disruption with the owner's horses. Jimmy provided the ranchers with his prime stock of Morgan race horses. And replaced the ones that had broken or damaged limbs."

I continued on with myself and my theories, "imagined, shipping drugs in their natural state, hay, along with Jimmy's prime race horses all over the country. Then I imagined they transported the injured horses with drugs to slaughter houses. The horses were eating it in it's natural state, which was the hay. The hay was ingested by the horses with broken limbs, and then were gutted before being slaughtered then incinerated. Now imagine hundreds of horse farms purchasing livestock from Jimmy, throughout the entire country. We're talking an empire of millions of dollars. This has been going on under our very noses for years and no one has ever suspected it. Even the hay in the goose neck trailer lose, who would ever suspect.

That's why Marie is the next target or victim. She's too close to what's happening. Jimmy may think she knows too much. After all, she had gone out with him for some time, years ago. Bill and Jimmy are afraid she'll figure it out, being the other best private investigator around.

Marie I'm sure will piece Lizabetty needing horses, then, Richard and Ralph shipping the new horses, and picking up the injured ones. Then Marie will piece together Rita's involvement with the both of them. Then finally my son, may have been killed for knowing what was on the video tapes. It was incriminating evidence about the horses and hay!"

My thoughts raced in my head, "Gosh! Marie's got to be the next victim! Maybe that's why she was shot in the first place. Will I get to tell her in time? Even if she's not hit tonight, she'll be aware of what I may have just figured out!"

I jumped in the fastest means of transportation known to man, my V-12 Lincoln machine, and darted furiously across town as I called Captain Sybinski in transit with my cell phone.

Meanwhile:

I had stopped at the drug store to pick up my cosmetic needs and photos, then continued home. Like Alec, I also had a long driveway, as I pulled into the driveway and stopped the car. Since there had been no one home for several days, the mail box was stuffed spilling some envelopes on the ground.

"Holy Moly," I said out loud, look at all the junk mail stuffed in there. I had one of those huge mail boxes that held a good amount of bulk mail. There was so much mail stuffed in the box I couldn't even carry it all. So, I made the necessary second trip back to the mailbox to get the rest, after leaving the first handful of mail on the front seat.

Abruptly, on the way back to the Viper with the second load of mail, I noticed my lawn lights casting a human shadow against the house, some distances away. "What the?" I said as I pulled out my little snub nose revolver. I wasn't expecting anyone, so I cautiously went up the windy drive. Slowly I approached my three-car garage and realized it was only Jimmy. I placed my revolver back into the holster and continued going about as usual.

Although I didn't see Jimmy, I saw his automobile was parked out of the way, close to the tree line at the rear of the drive, facing out. His headlights were off, but the glass from his headlights reflected my high beam rays. Clearly it was Jimmy's car, but I still didn't see Jimmy.

"He wouldn't just show up without calling," I thought. But, then again, he did call. Several times as a matter of fact, on the answering machine last night, when I chose not to return his calls because I was too tired.

I pushed the garage door remote opener, and I slowly continued to approach, wondering where Jimmy was. When suddenly, behind me I saw a car's headlights whipping up the driveway. I immediately stopped the Viper by the corner of the house. I stopped just before the first door of the three car garage, unable to see in the second door, where I usually park my Viper.

Alec was coming up the driveway, extremely fast. "What the heck?" I wondered, as I heard police cars some distance away.

Alec swerved directly in front of my Viper and jumped out of his car. His car continued to slowly roll and hit the garage, scraping his car's beautiful paint job. All this was happening within seconds.

He reached for his 38, as he ran towards me. I was so focused on what Alec was doing that I didn't realize I was being repeatedly shot at again.

"BANG! BANG! BANG!" as Alec jumped in front of me. Several gun shots were fired, as Jimmy, dressed in black, came out from the inside of my garage. I saw Jimmy's right hand drop something shinny.

"OH, NO!" I shouted. "Not again!" As I fell to the pavement from the gun fire, I was covered with blood on my face, my hands and clothes. Then Alec also fell directly in front of me.

"HELP, HELP I'M SHOT, I'M SHOT!" I shouted, as three police officers, including Captain Sybinski, hurried to help, with their guns drawn.

Gently they assisted me up to my feet and started to place me on a gurney getting ready to carry me off to the ambulance. But as the officers helped me stand, I stood before Alec, and then realized, I wasn't shot at all. It was Alec's blood splattered over my face and clothing! It was Alec who shielded my life as I looked down at the gapping cavities in the back of his chest. I couldn't believe what had just happened.

"Don't you die on me, you dummy!!" I shouted to Alec.

The EMTs swiftly took Alec into the ambulance, where I then saw Fuz, holding onto his father's hand. The police were securing the doors, as the ambulance rushed off. I wanted so much to thank him for what he did. No one has ever done for me as he has. I now knew, what he had gone through with David.

The Police had the cuffs on Jimmy, as well as Lieutenant Rockwell, who was sitting in one of the police cruisers. Alec was tough, really tough. He had said that to me, when he had me in his truck, rushing me to the hospital. I heard him, but I was too weak to answer him, last Tuesday. I turned my Viper around in my driveway and followed the ambulance to the Exeter Hospital. I drove slowly, wondering and wanting to know where Bill fit in this terrible ordeal. I started thinking all kinds of things, then I focused on what Alec had told me at his home. How all this came about and what he explained by the coffee table.

I was confident Alec would pull through. He was as tough as nails. I mean, they came no tougher. Besides, what would I do without him as my partner? He's my partner and he's the best darn associate any investigator could ever have. Words he himself always stated in front of me, about me.

I needed answers and I needed them fast, so I started with Sargent Fuz, right at the hospital. I wanted to know where the hell he was, during all this time. Both his father and I thought he had been terminated by the sniper, who we still didn't know.

Fuz came and sat by my side, holding back what I also felt inside. He put his arm around me, then said, "He'll be okay, Marie. The EMT's were doing a great job on the way over."

It was then I started directing, as the other half of our agency. I needed several things answered and until we were having our croissants back in the office together, this gas pump murder mystery caper wasn't over. As a matter of fact, this case was starting to really bug me.

Chapter XXII

The first question I asked Fuz, while we were sitting together was.

"Your father and I thought you were dead, killed by the sniper! Where the hell have you been?"

"Ms Quilby," Fuz said, "I was staying at my Grandma's house across town. Please let me explain. Dad and I viewed the tapes at Richard O'leahy's apartment last night. Dad offered to let me submit the evidence. That's how Pop helps me to achieve recognition at the precinct. He really didn't want any credit, he just wanted the ring leader, the people involved with shooting you, that's what he had told me. My dad has always kept me informed, in all your cases. But not as close as this one, and I believe he's talked to me about several of his cases. I called Lieutenant Rockwell that night after Dad left and I told the Lieutenant about the newly acquired video tapes, with incriminating evidence.

On the off shifts, the Lieutenant requires us to do that, to call him at anytime on any case, with any major evidence. This was his policy, and all of us went by it religiously. Anyway, I brought the Lieutenant up to date on the phone, as we do with all cases. However, instead of the usual procedure 'Tag 'em and Bag 'em', Then 'submit and record evidence' at the precinct, the Lieutenant said, "I'll be right over." Well, with that comment, "I'll be right over," and the way that Dad's been talking to me about the case, a giant red flag went up. I immediately became very suspicious. It was against procedures he himself implemented."

Alec had filled Fuz with all the details as they were investigating, including the woman with Bill, at the Wildfire club.

Fuz continued, "From the moment that the Lieutenant had said he would be right over, I knew I was tagged to be "dealt with in some way", so I took off and hid at Grandma's place. While out of sight, in hiding, I made many phone calls, regarding events that Dad had told me about. The first thing I did was check out the woman with Bill at the Wildfire. Come to find out, she provided Bill with the schedules. The schedules were of where and when Freaky Fred was transporting horses. This gave the Lieutenant time to get his supplier to ship special hay bails, which were just stored in plain horse trailers waiting for shipping at Jimmy Johnson estate. But this special hay was not to be eaten by the horses going to and fro.

The sold prime Morgan horses, which were going to the buyers, ate the regular hay also stored in the goose neck trailer. After watching the tapes again, and again from the apartment, I figured out that's what Richie was doing when he entered the horse trailer, while pumping gas. He made sure proper hay was being eaten by the correct horses. Quite an operation don't you think?"

"Yes Fuz," I replied. "If Alec didn't investigate the surmised flower pot, and the theory he had about Richie and a ransom, they may have gotten away with it. Was Colonel Davenport involved?"

"Big time Ms Quilby, but we can't prove it," Fuz said. "But, where else would Bill get and supervise the hay for shipping? The Colonel is the most logical explanation, I would think?"

Alec remained in very critical condition for a whole week, and the doctors were planning to have him stay there even longer.

I shuffled the events in my mind all week long, and then finally Alec was able to see visitors. Although family was the only visitors permitted, none according to the nurses ever showed, not even a phone call. I went to see him, wanting to know more about how he came to his conclusion.

"Hey, Alec, whasssup?" I cheerfully said, trying to lighten the situation.

Alec told me the entire scenario he theorized and manifested, then said, "Wait for me. Marie, we're dealing with an intelligent person, with no regard for any type of earthly life. Davenport's a cold blooded killer and devours everything that gets in his way. But, then again Marie, he added, he's never met someone like you."

"Oh, by the way Alec, I called Rita for you."

"Oh please Marie, why did you ever do that?"

"Cut the baloney Alec, go with the flow and knock it off," Marie replied.

"How's she doing?" Alec asked.

"Better than you. She's looking forward to meeting me at the Critter Creek Restaurant in Newington."

"How's Bill doing? To what degree was he involved?" Alec asked.

"Oh, he was involved alright, but we're finding out now, that he's been working undercover for the FBI. His involvement with the FBI is completely blown out of the water," I said.

"I guess I really screwed things up, didn't I Marie?" Alec said.

"Hold up, Alec, before you start ripping yourself down.

Number One: He knew we would find out eventually who was involved.

Number Two: When we were at the apartment, he had an opportunity to say that we were getting too close, and that we were going to blow his cover.

And now, finally, Number Three: There were no police, no FBI, and no undercover agents keeping an eye on Jimmy. Jimmy would have certainly taken my life if it weren't for you. So, cut the crap! Thank you for what you did."

"You're welcome, Marie. That's what partners are for, right? Shoot," Alec continued, "if Bill wasn't the sniper, then who the hell could it be? It's definitely one of the Colonel's boys for sure. Also, if he's still out there, you could still be in danger."

"This Davenport guy, you say he's from New England, Alec?"

"Yes."

"While you're in here, I'll do some research and obtain something to sink our teeth into."

"Tell Bill I said sorry about exposing the undercover operation, I'd like to see him, if it's at all possible, Marie."

"Okay, Alec, I'll see you tomorrow," I said.

Bill Rockwell's arrest didn't screw up anything. As a matter of fact, the bond between the Colonel and Bill became even stronger. One of the "Circle of Life" attorneys was assigned by the Colonel to get Bill out on bail. All Bill had to do was shut his mouth and let the attorney do all the talking. Bail was set for fifty thousand and the following day Bill was out on bail and roaming around like a proud peacock.

Angelo A. Fazio

Chapter XXIII

"Fuz, has Jimmy Johnson started unraveling yet?" I asked.

"No, not at all. His lips are sealed, in fear of what may happen to him. I'm still having a problem trying to understand why Jimmy would give up his horse racing empire, to deal with drugs," Fuz said. Gosh, the guy's a millionaire already. Why would he throw his entire career down the toilet? That doesn't make sense to me, unless somebody knows something we don't."

I felt this case wasn't some murder mystery that one reads about in a book, or watches on television. Each corner I turned, there was another obstacle, no longer a simple gas pump nozzle murder mystery. There was a lot of involvement with the FBI and who knows who else.

It was getting late and I thought I should visit Alec again, as he had done so many times for me.

"Alec," I said, gleaming my pearly whites, "you look great! How are you feeling this evening, my little Zucchini?"

"Your little Zucchini is fine. I feel wonderful," Alec said, under heavy medications.

"Why don't you spend the night here with me? What do ya think?"

He couldn't believe it. I jokingly started getting in under the sheets with him, causing him to blush somewhat.

"See, Mr. Black, you're okay," I said as I looked under the sheet.

"See everything works fine. Why don't you get out of this place and start doing something a little more constructive? Instead of lying around all day."

"I don't know, Marie. Maybe you can persuade the doctors with your charm. If it works, I'd leave with you in a minute," Alec said.

I then went out to speak with someone of importance and the doctor told me if he continues progressing, he would be out on Friday. Today was Wednesday. "Not bad," I thought. "It's been over a week since he got shot and he was doing great. No, not bad at all! Wow! He really is tougher than nails!"

I stayed at Alec's side most of the evening, playing cards and watching television, there was no question about it, I found him not only interesting, but also very intelligent and rather nice. Why I never got involved with Alec many years ago, is totally a mystery to me. He's not that good looking, but he's everything any woman would ever want. Why he and his wife separated, he has never said. I just hope this Rita woman doesn't hurt him like Olga Carbuncle has.

"So, you spending the night, Marie? This bed is certainly bigger than the back seat of the truck."

"I'd love to Alec, but I got to get going, I've got places to go and people to visit" I said.

"No problem," Alec replied.

There was definitely something wild and crazy between us. We kidded and joked around as friends much better than some married couples. How he controlled himself when we kidded with each other was again, another mystery.

The following morning, I went to the office to continue our work. It was Thursday, my turn to buy the treats. The only thing was, Alec wasn't here. I bought a croissant for myself, then read the paper and sipped my coffee. Moments later, there was a knock on the door.

"Come in," I said and then looked up.

"Rita!" I said, with surprise. "I wasn't expecting you back until tomorrow."

"I stored my Corvette in Pennsylvania and took the bus," Rita said.

"Well, that was a good idea," I said. "Usually people with sports cars don't drive them in the winter months anyway. I drive my Viper in the winter only because the streets in New Hampshire are always in perfect condition. Even after a snowstorm, the roads are down to bare pavement by the following day and even at times during the same day. Nice to see you Rita, sit down."

The office was still a little messy from a few weeks ago's burglary, but it still was impressive enough when one entered the door.

Rita looked around and then noticed the bullet hole through the window, and said, "Oh my Marie, they're after you too?"

"Yes, Rita, I was shot and left for dead, two and a half weeks ago, just like you Rita. I still can't believe it was Jimmy who shot you, but I guess it's true. Both

Alec and I agree however, that there may be another involved," I said.

"So, you and Jimmy were lovers also?" I asked.

"Yes," Rita answered.

"Did you ever meet his parents at all?" I asked.

"Oh yes, many times. I thought he was going to pop the marriage question on two occasions. But I guess I didn't fit his profile," Rita said. "His parents, who adopted Jimmy, thought the world of me, and thought I'd be good for him. Jimmy was always out there getting involved where he thought he belonged, instead of knowing where he fit. It was very difficult when Jimmy dumped me for another wealthier woman."

"Oh, my gosh," I thought. "I was the so-called, wealthier other woman! When I was with Jimmy, I had often heard him speak of another woman, but he never mentioned her name."

"So Jimmy was not their biological son?" I asked.

"Oh, no," Rita replied. "They couldn't have their own children, so they adopted. As I said, we were very close. I was especially close with Mrs. Johnson. She treated me as her daughter, and Jimmy and I weren't even married. She always wanted me to call her Helen. When their plane crashed, I grieved for several months. I missed her so very much."

"You don't mind if I ask you some questions about Jimmy, do you?"

"Of course not, Marie. I feel as though I've known you for some time. Jimmy always went out with women who fit the same type of profile. It took me a while to figure out who the wealthier women was. When I found out that you were that other woman, I never held it against you. The reason was that you're just as classy and pretty."

"Did Jimmy work or get an allowance, from his parents? Do you know?" I asked.

"Yes, I knew, like I said. I thought we were going to get married. Mr. and Mrs. Johnson gave him a salary of $1,000 a week, which I thought was very generous, for that time. But, Jimmy wanted more. He was kinda spoiled, if you know what I mean."

"Rita, what do you say, we go to the Critter Creek restaurant today, instead of tomorrow?"

"Sure, I don't mind," Rita said.

I guess I wasn't feeling very comfortable sitting in the office, where a second attempt on my life took place. Besides, it wasn't the same without Alec. Conversing in the restaurant around a multitude of people sounded safer. It was a nice restaurant over by the Newington shopping Mall.

We jumped in the car and drove off. When we arrived at the fancy restaurant, we went in and we ordered mouth watering steak tips and salmon. Up here we call it "Earth and Ocean food."

We continued chatting for a couple of hours. We talked about Jimmy, his parents, and close friends. When we finished chatting, I suggested we go visit Mr. B.

"Do people really call him that?" Rita asked.

"Yes, they do. There was "Mr. B" way before they had "Mr. Tee" on television." I said with a smile.

I informed her that Alec was getting out of the hospital tomorrow and she got all "googly".

Alec had no idea that Rita was coming to visit. I was hoping he wouldn't be upset with me. When we arrived at his room, Alec was just coming out of the Bat Cave.

"Hey, Alec, look who I bumped into," I said.

"Hi, Alec," Rita said.

"Hi, Rita, I see you're mending nicely," Alec replied.

"I'm sorry about what I said in Pennsylvania," she said. "If I hadn't been involved with Richie, things may have been different, for sure."

"Rita, the thing is, you were involved with Richie and you cheated on him and you used me."

"Like I said Alec, I'm sorry," she said sadly, as she turned and walked towards the door.

Alec looked over at me as to say, what shall I do? And said to Rita, "Rita, where are you going?"

She turned with swelled watering eyes and said, "That night at the Wildfire was the nicest night I had in a while."

I knew then, Rita didn't mean to hurt my feelings by saying what she did, in Pennsylvania, that she was using me. She, in fact, must have had some feelings to remember our night at the Wildfire Club.

"Why don't we all show our battle shot wounds?" I blurted out, changing the sensitive atmosphere. And we all laughed.

Rita said laughingly in between each word. "Maybe, we should all wear bulletproof vests!"

"I guess we all have had our share of lickings," I said.

"So big deal, Rita had an 'affair' while being with Richard O'leahy. Big Deal, how wrong could it be? The affair was with me."

Rita and I stayed a while longer before Alec asked, "Marie, can you please pick me up in the morning?"

When I replied Alec's favorite saying, "No problem" I was trying to tease him and his odd sayings.

The following morning, I picked up Alec at the hospital and we sailed off to the office, for more punishment from these "Fools in New England".

Angelo A. Fazio

Chapter XXIV

Marie had explained to me all of the circumstances, which had taken place, while I was tied up in the hospital. Bill never showed his face at the hospital, but I think it was because he didn't want to blow his cover again. So, he didn't dare come and visit.

I looked around the office and started making arrangements to have the windows fixed. I called the insurance company and got credit from the standard windows, then applied the credit amount along with other moneys, into bulletproof windows. I felt we needed obstructions. We didn't need to get shot at again, like little ducks at a shooting gallery.

I sensed that Marie liked the new me. During the past ten years, she'll be the first to tell you, I had become a tightwad, never agreeing to spend much in the office. I always kept things in the thrifty mode, cheap! That all changed, while I was stuck in the infirmary.

I asked Marie to call Fuz. We needed Fuz to work on Jimmy's background and also to find out what Jimmy spent his money on. I also asked Marie if we could allocate several thousands of dollars to install a new security alarm system. Burglars weren't going to be able to ransack our office again without the fear of loud, nerve-racking, piercing alarms.

Now that we knew that Lieutenant Bill Rockwell was an undercover FBI agent, it cast a whole new horizon of possibilities. When I called Bill on the phone, I let him have it. I gave him a good tongue lashing for not telling us, or at least me, of his undercover operations. I would have never gone detecting in his direction looking for answers, if I had known.

"Phooey!" I thought. "What a waste of my tiny brain cells, working hard in the wrong direction. If only he had told me."

However, since he hadn't told me, I treated him as one of them.

Marie indicated that she was purchasing another computer, solely for the purpose of old files, instead of the cabinet systems we endured for the last twenty-two years.

Yes, we were back, and back with a brand new attitude.

"Are you alright, Alec?" Marie asked in concern.

"Oh, I get it. You think I've flipped out. No, no, I'm fine Marie. I've finally come to my senses. We could have been shot and killed at any time. It's not like years ago, when people got together and talked out their differences. No, the way people resolve a problem today is, they shoot and kill it. Well, not if I can help it. Each time I look at the bullet hole through the window, it sends shivers down my spine. You mean more to me than just a detective. You're, you're my, well, you know what I'm trying to say. I hope you feel the same," I said.

"Yes, Alec, I know what you're trying to say," Marie smiled.

"Is there something you would like to add to the security of this office?" I asked.

"No," Marie said, "you're doing just fine, Alec."

"If you think of anything, just buy it, okay?" I said.

After getting mentally orientated, Marie called Rita. Marie and I needed to know more about Jimmy. We asked Rita to meet at the Garden Gate restaurant, just outside of Dover on route 108.

Marie, like me, doesn't like to be used. Jimmy J. screwed up big time, especially when he tried shooting Marie in her own yard. Wrong decision on his part. What the hell was he thinking? You don't screw with Marie, or me, and expect to get away with it. We knew that Jimmy would be out on bail soon, because the Colonel knows too many people in high places. Plus, the Colonel has a reputation of having the best attorneys in the world. So, that meant that Marie and I had to work fast. We jotted down questions that needed answers and decided the one person who was able to help us was Rita.

We met Rita at Garden Gate Restaurant and Marie did all the asking.

"Hi, Rita," Marie said as she entered the restaurant door. Rita reciprocated the greeting. The hostess seated us, then Marie went on, "Since you knew Jimmy much longer than I did, I figured perhaps your answers would really help us resolve many of the unanswered questions."

The waitress came and took our orders then went to her business.

"Go ahead, Marie," Rita said. "I'll do the best I can to help."

"When did you first meet Jimmy?"

"We met in college, Northern State College," she said. "I studied teaching, while Jimmy majored in Accounting. During the first couple of years, I didn't think Jimmy was going to make it. It wasn't until the second semester, of the second year, when he started getting good grades. One of his professors, who had come from England, took a lot of interest in him and helped him through college."

With that sentence, Marie noticed that I was squinting my eyebrow. I usually do that when I'm deep in thought, I think she realized it and she figured that something was afoot. She then went on to ask, "Did he ever do drugs while in college?"

"There were many students in college who tried it back then. But, I never got involved with any of it. Yes, it was around that same time frame when Jimmy started doing drugs, and he also started doing better with his grades," Rita said.

Marie asked other questions, but I had what we needed to do some background work. I continued listening, while Rita talked. Rita was very interesting to listen to.

About twenty minutes had elapsed, when our waitress arrived with our awesome meal. Now I knew why Garden Gate had such a great reputation, It was a family owned restaurant and they served food in that fashion. It was a well prepared delicious meal, and there was enough food to feed an entire family of six.

We finished our lunch and decided to split in opposite directions. Marie sped off with Rita, asking other questions about Jimmy, while I headed in a different direction.

Several things that Rita had said just weren't settling comfortably in my mind. I figured that between what she had said earlier and what she stated at the restaurant table, something was definitely going on.

I went back to the office and I started working with a special website concerning England. I also called Fuz and asked him for another favor pertaining to Northern State College. Yes, there was something definitely afoot alright.

Angelo A. Fazio

Chapter XXV

When I got home, late in the afternoon, I called Maureen, Lieutenant Bill Rockwell's wife. She sounded somewhat angry, especially when I said that it was me who was calling. She gave me a feeling of being ashamed of myself for getting her Bill in trouble. I was trying to be understanding, thinking perhaps she herself didn't know of Bill's undercover activities. But as I was thinking that, I said to myself, "I'm not about to take any bullcrap from anyone, even Maureen."

"Maureen," I said, "where and when can I meet Bill? It's very important that I see him."

"I have no idea where he is, Alec," she replied.

"Could you give him this message when he arrives? Have him call me at my home, at any time. I need to meet with him. Also, don't let him call from your home, it may be bugged."

"Okay, I'll give him the message," she said.

I had just finished eating for the evening and I was about to do the dishes when the phone rang. It was Marie.

"Alec," she said, "Rita told me that Jimmy and his step-father didn't get along. They didn't get along at all."

"Yeah," I said.

"I myself have been thinking overtime on our "dear old friend", Jimmy as well. However, this is no place or time to talk about it. I know where you're going with this information Marie, and fortunately I agree with you. Can we talk about it in the morning? I'm expecting a very important call from Bill right now. At any second. I have a hunch he'll be seeing the Colonel shortly about moving some drugs. I'll let you know when I know. I gotta meet with him before the Colonel does. And oh yes Marie, one other thing, I got Fuz to do a little research on a certain professor at Northern State College, who came from England. Find out if Fuz has got anything yet. We'll talk later. I gotta hang up in case Bill calls. Ciao Cara Mia." I said speaking in one of my several languages.

"Call me as soon as you get something," Marie said.

Here it was, a little after nine and still no word from Bill. I was kind of getting concerned. I started watching television for a while to help get my mind off of things. I was almost falling asleep, when the phone started ringing. I looked at the clock on the wall and it said half past nine.

I answered the phone, "Hello?"

"I heard that you have been looking for me?" Bill asked.

"Yeah," I replied.

"What do you want?" he said.

"We need to talk, Bill." I said.

"What are you trying to do, Alec, get me killed?"

"No, on the contrary, you big dope! I'm trying to see you in a quiet place where no one is listening or watching. This whole undercover thing is going to blow-up in your face, with this new information I collected. Please Bill, meet me somewhere. But, before you say anything more, first hang up and call from a pay phone. If you are, don't tell me your location. Just tell me, in our old "code", where we can meet."

"What's going on Alec, our old code? The code we three had, back in the Service?" Bill asked.

"Yes, Bill," Alec said.

It took a while for Bill to remember the code sequence, but he sent the address and time over the phone line. We continued talking briefly and within a few seconds of giving me the code, we heard a click, as though someone was listening.

"That must be the FBI listening!" Bill said, in surprise.

"You mean you're calling from home!?" Alec said.

"No, I'm calling from the pay phone, across the street."

"Crap, Bill! Like they don't have that phone tapped also," I said.

I was thankful that no one knew our special method of communicating. It was a simple system that only three people knew, only because we three created it, back then. I also told him to dress in silence.

"Catch you later, Bill," I said as we hung up.

Bill sent the coded message, to meet at my parent's farm, out back by the horse stables. It was the same place where my son Fuz had hidden from the Colonel's elite rifleman.

His coded message read:
11,5,14,20,19,20,18,5,5,20. 13; 2300,13,20.
Which decoded spelled out:
Kent Street#13@23:00 Military time.

Each letter represented a number up to twenty-six. The number after the period was the number of the dwelling. The numbers after the semicolon represented Military time, and to dress in camouflage.

It was just a simple code and very easy to comprehend.

It was now 9:45 pm. My parent's place was about 20 minutes away. There was plenty of time to check with Fuz and find out what information he had found.

I called him and he told me what he had found out. Jimmy Johnson was in fact adopted. He also spent a lot of time and money with a Professor from Northern State. This particular professor had been accused of dealing drugs, but it never was proven in court, and the case was thrown out of court because of insufficient evidence.

The professor came from Dover, England. He moved to the Greater Boston area, back in the later 70's. He had come to this country with impressive doctorate credentials in Accounting and Chemistry.

Doctor Johnson applied for employment at Northern State College, and he was welcomed with open arms, filling a previous professor's position.

There was only one thing that I wasn't able to put my finger on, but I was hopeful that I would solve that question before another person would get hurt or killed.

It was now 10:00 pm, and I wanted to be at the designated place, much earlier than Bill. I wanted to comb the area and make sure we were alone.

I called Marie to let her know what I knew. Then I went on my way to the meeting place, which was my parent's farm, located just outside of Exeter.

Angelo A. Fazio

Chapter XXVI

While Alec was at his meeting with Bill, I wasn't going to sit idle.

Especially, while I knew Alec was out there, after just coming out of the hospital. I remembered back to just two weeks ago when I was on my first day back on the job, right out of the hospital. I remembered how difficult it was for me. I was in pain, very tired and too stubborn to admit it. I was sure that Alec was feeling somewhat the same, I already knew he was stubborn.

I was about ready to leave my home, to do some surveillance work at Jimmy's place, before he got out on bail, when the phone rang. I paused a moment and debated whether or not to pick it up.

"But, what if it's Alec calling back," I thought, and decided to pick up the phone.

"Hello?"

"Ms Quilby," the voice said, "I'm at the police station. You got to come and see this." It was Sargent Fuz.

I told him what his father was up to and where he was going.

When he said, "There's enough time. Hurry, it's very important."

When I arrived and drove up to the police station, Fuz immediately came rushing out to the car. He had paperwork in one hand and bulletproof vests in the other.

"What the heck is all this?" I asked, as he jumped into the car.

"Don't laugh about the vests," he said. "Rita called and told me to make sure you and Dad wear vests everyday until this is all over. I guess she has the hots for Dad, and also considers you to be a friend."

"So, what cha got?" I asked.

"I looked up the articles that Dad had asked me about. The Professor, come to find out, has a very shady and a questionable background. It goes back to when Jimmy attended Northern State College. This Professor Johnson was nearly convicted for pushing drugs. They threw his case out of court, but the students who were involved with the drugs were either expelled or had served time of probation. The students had statements, all pointing the finger at the Professor as the drug provider."

"Yeah, so," I said.

"Well, I jotted down their names and addresses and made official police work of it. After some research, for further information, I had found two of the students that were involved with drugs at Northern State, and I called them on the phone. Both students knew each other and also hated Professor Johnson's guts. They claim that he ruined their careers and their lives. Both students stated that the Professor always invited students who he supplied drugs to, to his place often. At that time, he had a farm in Salisbury, but his farm had no animals. There were just fields and fields of hay for the other farmers who did have animals. During the hay season, the students helped bail and load trucks and trailers of hey."

"You don't have to tell me the rest, Fuz. I know where you're going with this," I said.

"Okay, Ms Quilby, but did you know that Jimmy is out on bail?" He asked.

"Whoa!! That was a little tidbit of information that's something Alec and I didn't know." I said, "thanks for sharing Fuz."

We left to meet Alec, at his parent's farm. We had to bring him up with the information that Fuz had acquired, especially the fact that Jimmy was out on bail.

"I guess the old saying is true," I said to Sargent Fuz.

"What's that?" He replied.

"Have you ever heard the old expression, 'Money talks and bullcrap walks?' I guess you can get anybody out on bail if you have the money."

"I can't say that I haven't heard that," Fuz replied.

Sargent Fuz was right, there was plenty of time when we approached the farm.

The Black's Estate had two driveways. One driveway went directly to the farm house and the other went to the chicken houses and stables, which were about a quarter of a mile apart. I had never been to Alec's parent's place, in all the time I've known him. Wow! This place was huge!

We drove to the farm house to make it seem as though the old folks were having company, in the event that someone was watching. But we never knocked or entered the home. We just parked the car in their driveway and we quietly advanced to the area where we though Alec would be.

It was dark, almost pitch black out, sort of like the blackout in the nineteen sixties. But, Sargent Fuz, from an infant, grew up here on the Estate, and he knew the entire topography of the terrain. He knew every contour, up and down. He would know where not to bump into trees, and know where to walk and not walk. He even knew where a small body of water was for the horses to drink from.

I never knew Alec came from big money. Sargent Fuz told me there were thousands and thousands of square yards of farm land. Why Alec never got involved with his family's estate or the millions of dollars in equity, is another mystery. All I knew of, was the upstairs "junk room" at Alec's house, as he called it. Unless Alec, himself, wants to talk about it, I will never talk or go to that subject.

We continued walking and finally stopped. We sat on the ground trying to get our night vision acclimated. Alec had always talked about night vision, and until now, I had no reason to acquire the ability or use it. I was told to look through the sides of my eyes and not look directly at any object. After a brief period of time, I noticed I could see quite well.

Sargent Fuz suddenly whispered, "Marie, don't jump. My Dad's a few inches away from you, and you have your hand on his arm."

I immediately lifted my hand and said, "How come you can see him, and I can't?" I really couldn't see him and I didn't realize that I had touched his arm. I thought it was a tree branch.

"Because Dad taught me how," He said.

Then I heard, "Marie, what are you doing out here?"

"We came out with information, and a vest for you. You're going to get hurt," I said. I caused Alec to chuckle. "Where are you? I can see your son, but why can't I see you?"

I suddenly jumped when I felt his lips touch my cheek. "Hey! I nearly jumped out of my skin when you kissed my cheek! I still don't see you, you dummy," I said.

"Good," Alec replied. "If no one can see me, then no one can shoot me."

I then asked, "Is Bill here yet?"

"No, not yet."

"What do you want to see him for?" I asked.

"Shh, here he comes," he said.

"Wow!" I said in a whisper and reached out for Alec's arm. "I can see him coming. Night vision really works. But, where the hell are you?"

Sargent Fuz responded, "He left already Marie, if you look about five feet to the right of Bill you'll see Pop."

"That's Alec?" I said. "You mean, I was just reaching out to a tree limb?"

I could see the both of them, but then they both disappeared. Everything was still for about fifteen minutes or so, when I heard rifle shots, just like when Rita was hit. The rifle, like Alec had said, had a silencer on it. This time however, I could see the gun flare. It was pretty dark, and I managed to see a slight flash.

I told Sargent Fuz to go to the car, and call for back up. We never carried the cell phones out because on night maneuvers or stakeouts, if we forget to turn the ringer off and the phone rings, it can give your position away and who knows what could happen?

I slowly manipulated my way over to where the gun flashes were, thinking perhaps I could cuff the sniper. It took some time to get there, though. When I got to the area where I saw the gunfire flash, I stopped. At this spot, I could see much, much more than from where we were. I could clearly see Bill, but I didn't see Alec.

"Maybe after the gunfire, they separated?" I wondered. Suddenly, I noticed Bill heading towards the horse stables in a crouching position.

So far, only two shots were fired, and I knew the shots that were fired came from this general area where I currently was. Was the sniper shooting at Bill, or maybe the both of them? Could this have been an ambush getting the both of them here in one spot? Alec had mentioned to me about the tapped pay phone line. What if the people listening were not the FBI? What if it was one of the Colonel experts? Who knows what type of military surveillance equipment he may have acquired over the years. Maybe the Colonel tapped the lines?

There was no doubt in my mind, Alec was right. The Colonel had to be behind this. Why would the FBI shoot at Bill, one of their own?

"Gee, I hope the police back up comes soon," I thought.

All of a sudden without warning, I saw a huge, big fat guy emerge from the horse stables. He was about 75 feet away from where I was stationed.

I viewed the big fat guy, with two others holding guns. It looked like Jimmy, but how could Jimmy have known where Alec and Bill were? They waved their guns for Bill and a camouflaged man, who I think was Alec, to go into the barn.

I finally got a glimpse of the two of them. Suddenly, I was caught by surprise again, the ground started to shake a bit and move, about twenty feet ahead of me.

"Holy Crap!!" I thought to myself. It was extremely frightening! A person in full camouflage stood up in front of me. I was in total dismay, thinking he saw me there, as he then walked right near me, not noticing that I was sitting there.

My heart was pounding and pounding away, beating like a drum, so hard and loud. How could he have missed me? Now I finally understood what Alec's military friends meant about, the enemy unable to see you.

As the big Jamoke, who had just got up in front of me, walked to the barn, I followed him, but from some distance away. I wanted to stay undetected. I watched him as he reached the barn door and then went into the barn into a dimly lit area.

I continued to follow him slowly and I reached the barn door on the opposite end of the barn. I continued making my way up front to where they were all conversing.

When I got to a certain point, I stopped. I was about thirty feet away when I recognized one of the people from Alec's photo. I recognized the fat man, it definitely was The Colonel.

The horses were moving around in the stalls, shuffling the hay, making my advancing movement sounds unnoticeable. Plus, the horses were making snorting noises. Which also helped. Finally I was in the stall directly behind the Jamoke, the guy I had followed in.

I stayed quiet and listened hard to what was going on. The Colonel had planned to inject drug overdoses, into both Bill and Alec. He said they'd bring the dead bodies back to Alec's place and plant all kinds of incriminating evidence on them.

Where Alec lived pretty much in the woods, it would be so easy to do.

"Where was Sargent Fuz? Where was the back up?" I wondered, as my mind raced.

There was Jimmy, The Colonel, The Professor, and the unknown guy standing before me with the camouflage outfit, with a rifle in hand.

The Colonel had just finished injecting Bill and was approaching Alec.

I started thinking about how Alec had run into harm's way for me and saved my life. And I, I could do nothing. I continued to stay completely motionless, almost like frozen in place, when suddenly out of nowhere, everything that happened next, happened so naturally.

As I was thinking, "Where's Fuz with the back up?" I just couldn't sit still any longer and jumped out of the stall that I was hiding in.

"Where's the freaken back up?!" I shouted, as I disarmed the Jamoke in the Camouflage outfit.

"Where is the freaken back up?" I shouted again and continued with my left elbow bone jabbing the big guys right eye. The big Jamoke started whimpering like a baby. My Karate instincts came into full blown bloom.

The Colonel watched my movements and tried desperately to inject me with an over dose, as I was dealing with the big Jamoke. I went down into a split and the colonel injected the Jamoke directly into the side of the chest.

Jimmy fired his gun directly at me as I slid under the Colonels crotch. Alec hit Jimmy, while his hands were tied, causing the bullet to hit the Colonel.

While Alec worked on Jimmy, with his hands tied, I came around the backside of the Colonel and Karate kicked the Professor right in the testicles. The Professor grasped his testicles and went down like a sack of potatoes, which then gave me time to wrench and remove Jimmy's gun. The Colonel who was hit on the left thigh had started bleeding very heavily.

"Jimmy may have hit his major artery," I thought. The Colonel with all his weight went off his feet like a ton of horse manure.

"The bigger they are, the harder they fall," I said with a rhythm. "Where's the back up?" Marie shouted loudly, relentlessly working the bodies of the evil doers.

"You guy's think you're tough? Huh? Huh?" Marie kept shouting. "Well, you haven't met Marie, Marie Quilby!" Marie said, as she kept kicking the crap out of these guys.

As I heard and watched Marie, I felt like I was viewing Marie in a musical performance, but with an extremely deadly beat. She moved so gracefully with such unbelievable speed. Her hands were like steel swords as she pulverized their manly physiques. Marie was my partner, and I loved it! She continued on, hurting Jimmy and the Colonel, beating them to what I had considered mercilessly. Marie in fact more than just astonished me, she astounded me to no end.

"It's about time" Marie said as the back up finally arrived. They rushed Bill into an ambulance first because of his condition and immediately took him to the hospital. They then started loading me into an ambulance. Jimmy had managed to rip open my gunshot wounds, on my chest again, just before Marie could reach Jimmy. As I looked back I then watched Marie give Jimmy the worst karate chop you can imagine, knocking him completely off of his feet and onto the ground, saying, "You can hurt me you jerk, but when it comes to you hurting my Alec, nobody!"

As she hit him again and again, "that's right, nobody, is going to hurt my Alec!" She proclaimed.

Clearly, as I looked back from the ambulance, Marie was no one to fool around with. She in fact was a walking artillery unit, a kag of Dynamite with a short fuse, in life threatening situations.

Angelo A. Fazio

Chapter XXVII

Sargent Fuz, and I were at the farm for some time. We collected lots of evidence, unlike the few drops of blood that Alec had collected at the fuel station, at the beginning of this fiasco three weeks ago. We were determined to make this case stick.

The Homicide department, along with the crime department, followed procedure and again placed the yellow ribbon approximately an acre around the barn, of the current crime scene. This time, however, since we were directly involved with the crime, I didn't feel pressured into leaving. With Bill and Alec on their way to the hospital, we managed to collect bullet casings and bullet slugs that we found imbedded in hay bails and also into the wooden posts. We had the Colonel and his gang of fools dead to rights. Fuz and I collected the syringe and drugs that were induced. We collected "the whole nine yards".

We even collected the slug that had been lodged in the Colonel's leg, after they removed it from him while in the hospital.

I went to the office and stayed up the whole night, and tried placing all the pieces together. I found out that Jimmy had a very dysfunctional background. It was too bad, with all his education and money. You'd think he would be the happiest man on the planet.

"How could I be so fooled involving myself with Jimmy?" I wondered. "Trust in no one, is my new motto. Well, except for Alec that is."

Two days had passed, and Alec recovered from his set back and was right back on top of the case.

I can't believe his determination and strength. Together we saw it through.

"Good morning, Marie," he said as he entered the door with the morning coffee and newspapers.

"What's up?" I asked. "Where's the croissants?"

"You're not going to believe this, Marie. I guess there are others now who find croissants appealing. Peggy's bakery was fresh out this morning," he said.

Before we started reading the paper, I had a lot of questions to clear up, beginning with Jimmy. No man has ever baffled me as Jimmy had. The way we shared the most intimate affections and total trust. The way I submitted myself totally, to someone I thought I knew nearly everything about.

"Alec, what did you find out about Jimmy, that you didn't tell me?" I asked.

"Marie, I could never, ever, get involved with your love life. Marie, I really liked Jimmy. I thought he'd be the one for you. I'm sorry about the way things turned out for you. Who was I, to try and convince you, that he had a shady background? Fuz told me of his shady past. After he tried shooting you at your home, I was hoping you'd find out on your own so you wouldn't think of me as being jealous or a mean person."

"Well, cough it up, Alf," I said.

"We'll have to go back quite a few years," Alec said, "back to when Jimmy was in college. Then I'll tie in how the Colonel came into all this. Well, as you know, Jimmy wasn't doing all that well in college, as Rita had mentioned. When Professor Johnson took an interest in Jimmy, the Professor had an ulterior motive for taking Jimmy under his wing. Professor Johnson needed Jimmy's parents, and the Morgan Race Horse Empire, to flow and flood the underworld drug market. I didn't find out about this, until Sargent Fuz did some heavy background research recently.

James Johnson, Jimmy's adoptive dad, was related to the Professor Johnson. He was the same Professor Johnson that lived in Dover, England. With all of his credentials, he came to America and got established, as you know. Well, they were brothers. Jimmy's adoptive father and Professor Johnson were brothers. They were brothers that didn't get along with one another. In fact, they hated each other, because one was more successful than the other. I know that may sound ridiculous, but it was a fact, according to Scotland Yard. When the Professor realized that Jimmy was his brother's adopted son, he started working the ultimate plan. The Professor's plan of getting Jimmy involved into drugs may have also accounted for Jimmy's possible passing grades, acquired during the last two years at Northern State College. The Professor also needed a method of transporting the drugs. The Professor's ambitions had only one problem, James and Helen Johnson, Jimmy's adoptive parents. Jimmy's parents didn't want anything to do with his brother from England, especially with transporting drugs. It wasn't too long after that, during a trip, when tragedy struck. James Johnson, Jimmy's folks from New Hampshire, were taking a flight out to visit the parents for Christmas, in Dover, England. While traveling on the plane, on the trip out, the plane crashed into the Atlantic Ocean.

Fuz discovered, from the Professor, that Jimmy had something to do with the disappearance of his parent's private plane. The Professor acquired the knowledge of a bomb set in the airplane, which Jimmy had set to go off over the ocean. Jimmy accidentally told the Professor this top secret information while he was under the influence of the drugs. Jimmy needed money for drugs. Jimmy wanted all the money and the inheritance, not just the allotted allowance his father was giving him.

When the Professor got wind of his finance status and what he did, he saw an opportunity to blackmail Jimmy. If he didn't use his horse farm to transport drugs and substances like hay, he'd report him to the authorities.

That's how Jimmy got involved way over his head. Like Rita said, he was always poking into places where he didn't belong.

After Jimmy's inheritance got involved with the transportation of the drugs, the Professor infiltrated the college campuses and the drugs spread, just as quickly as it did in the armed forces. Drugs spread in New England colleges, like wild fire. It took off like a nuclear blast out in the Nevada Desert. The market exploded. And the Professor's plans increased drug circulation. The Professor told Fuz and Lieutenant Rockwell, what better way to contaminate society, than through a portion of the young generation in college, especially New England Colleges?

Now that Jimmy was deeply involved, moving drugs and beginning dealings with the West Coast, California, he became even more fearful of the Professor. He was blackmailing Jimmy for thousands of dollars. All because of the knowledge of the bomb in his parent's plane.

Now Colonel Davenport knew Professor Johnson when he was stationed in the military over in Europe. Germany was where we were stationed before we had orders to go to Vietnam. The Colonel got involved with drugs about six months before we were shipped out.

Colonel Davenport and I, before that time, took off on test flights every weekend. The aircrafts, after minor repairs, needed Pilots to test the crafts before placing them back on duty. The Colonel and I were going all over Europe, Spain, Italy, France, and England. You name the country, we were there, until one weekend when he started going off on his own to England.

After that very first weekend, I was assigned to Caption Rateliff, until the Colonel and I joined again in Nam.

The reason why I say all this, is because, during the early years, when I knew the Colonel, he was as straight as an arrow. It was about midway into my six-year hitch, when his personality started changing. He started with this "Circle of Life" bullpucky, which didn't really mean a damn thing, until we were several months into Nam.

That's why I wanted to see Bill alone at my parents farm. Bill was in serious trouble, meeting the Colonel during their next meeting. I was going to tell Bill that the Colonel knew of his undercover FBI operation.

His girlfriend, the woman at the Wildfire club, worked directly for the Colonel and she knew Bill was still involved with the FBI. I was going to tell him that the next time he was to meet with the Colonel, to make sure he had adequate back-up. I also was going to mention the Professor's and Jimmy's tie in together. I also wanted to mention that a combination of things may occur during his next visit with the Colonel, but I never got the chance. Somehow they knew of our meeting at my parents farm? Never did I ever expect them at my family's place! They certainly did ambush us both."

After Alec and I chatted, we called Bill to make sure he was recovering well, and then we went on with our loose ends.

Chapter XXVIII

It was truly amazing that Marie was able to use her martial arts abilities. It had been three years since Marie's last trophy accomplishment, after many years of training and traveling to endless competitions in the US.

"Holy mackerel, Marie," I said. "I have never seen anyone move with such amazing skills in Karate. And believe me, I've known many men who have used it. I was totally impressed by the way you took control in the horse barn, the condition there was definitely fatal for Bill and I. You took a most dreadful situation and neutralized the circumstances. You handled the four of them, as though it were nothing at all!"

Marie laughed and said, "Yeah, right."

"Yes, Marie I mean it. I couldn't even see your hands move! All I saw were bodies falling all over the place!"

"Stop it. You'll give me a big head," she said, in her German accent. "Hey, get back to the conversation! Who was that guy in that camouflage get up, that scared the heck out of me?" Marie asked.

"Let me finish where I left off first Marie. As I was saying, the Colonel got involved with Professor Johnson in England, and when we all got out of the service, we went our separate ways. However, the Colonel and his 'circle of life' was still going strong. When the Colonel found an opportunity or opening here in the education systems, he reached Professor Johnson in England and asked him to apply at Northern State College. That's how they got together again."

"Alec who was the other Jamoke in the camouflaged outfit?" Marie inquired again.

The question she asked, was the most difficult question I had to answer for Marie. It was something I've lived with since I left the Military.

"That Jamoke, as you refer to him as, was David." I muttered. "That sumbitch never did die in my arms." It was hard to say it, but it finally came out.

"Apparently, during our last mission in Vietnam, where our helicopter was under severe artillery fire, I was hit through my stomach three times. I was hit and bleeding badly. Just before getting out of range of gun fire with the chopper, David stepped in harm's way to protect my life. That final bullet the enemy expired, struck David down. Yes, David was struck with the deadly force and he landed in my arms. He died in my arms as I remembered, as we flew off in the helicopter.

Bill also thought he was dead. Although, in reality, I was the one who blanked out from losing so much blood. As I understand the situation now, Bill was sitting in the front of the chopper. How could Bill really have known, he actually died? I always thought David died in my arms taking a bullet for me. But though he was shot, he wasn't shot as bad as I. David still had his vitals and survived, where I, from losing so much blood, I totally blacked out.

I lived with a guilty feeling all of my life. The Colonel had led us all to believe that David had died. I guess after David recovered, he became the Colonel's gopher. He was his personal sniper sort to speak. Perhaps the Colonel needed David to move freely in the underworld. He wanted to use a dead man's name and his deadly force, to be able to shift in and out of society without question, when it came to legal confinements.

There was nothing to link the Colonel with any deaths that had occurred during the transition into the United States. This process of transition, according to Sargent Fuz, was the Colonel getting professor Johnson into the states and it took almost a decade to accomplish. I think if Lieutenant Rockwell looks back, he may find that the opening at Northern State College may have been provided by some sort of accident of some nature.

I feel I was betrayed by David's deceit and angered by all he's put me through. All these years living with all the guilt." I said, "but can you imagine, Marie, this multi-million dollar drug lord captured by us? Merely because of a couple of blood droppings."

I looked at Marie with my best smile and asked, "Marie, may I take you out to celebrate tonight?"

"Well," she said, "what do you have in mind, Mr. Black?"

"I was thinking of taking you some place really nice.

A place I've heard so much about.

A place I'd love to share with you, Marie. For years I have often wanted to take you out, without fear of losing you as my partner.

A place called Fazio's Cuisine. Then perhaps, maybe share a few drinks, do a little dancing, and who knows, whatever happens, happens."

"Oooooh, that place?" Marie said, in her accent.

"I've also heard so much about that place. Only thing Alec, I've been up all night and I'm very tired. So, sorry, I don't think so." Marie said.

With that, I went back to reading the morning paper and commented again on how Peggy's Bakery had run out of croissants.

Suddenly to my surprise, Marie said, "Alf, I wasn't interested in going out, but. I didn't say anything about, you not coming over. We can order a few things out, and you can pick it up, while I slip into something a little more comfortable. We could have a few drinks, set some music down low, and have a dance or two. Who knows? I may not fall asleep while in your company. See, you dummy, it doesn't take much to make me feel content."

I knew Marie was very tired from being up all night. So I said, "What do ya say, Marie? Why don't we knock off for the day?"

When she replied, "Alec, it's only 11:00am in the morning. Are you sure?"

"Yeah, I'm sure," I said. "We own the detective agency, don't we? We can take time off if we want and when ever we want."

Marie smiled and said, "I'm going home to rest for tonight."

Then said, "Thank you for the flowers, Alec."

"What do ya mean?" I asked.

"The sweetheart roses that you bought me," Marie said.

"You mean you knew I bought them for you and not Jimmy?" I asked.

"Of course you dummy," Marie said as she laughed and headed towards the office door, "see ya later alligator."

"What an amazing woman," I thought. "How can I ever tell her that?"

As Marie drove away, the clouds again started shifting in, which only meant one thing, cold and rain, cold and windy, cold and snow, snow, snow.

After our totally unforgettable evening, we met at the office the following morning.

"Good morning, Marie," I said, as she entered the door three minutes before nine.

"Good morning, Alec," Marie replied, as she looked directly into my eyes without blinking and smiled scrunching her nose, giving me the feeling she had a fun time last night.

THE END?

About the Author

Angelo Fazio "Faz" was born and raised in Georgetown, Massachusetts. He joined the military at age eighteen and served for six years during the Vietnam conflict. He now resides in the beautifully scenic state of New Hampshire with his lovely wife. He also has two grown children and two wonderful grandchildren.